CW00828407

Change of Seasons

by

J. L. McDonough

Orcadian Press
Richmond, Indiana

Published by Orcadian Press, Richmond, Indiana 47374

ISBN-978-0-692-47014-5

CONTENTS

Chapter One: Winter Romance, Summer Love 7

Chapter Two: Three Sets 49

Chapter Three: A Night at the Movies 75

Chapter Four: Autumnal Equinox 85

Chapter Five: Winter Solstice 97

Chapter Six: A Season in New York 133

Chapter Seven: Return of Spring 185

CHAPTER ONE

Winter Romance, Summer Love

1.

Pulling the tavern door closed behind him, David struggled through the Friday evening, after-work crowd to the bar where Harry was waiting. He squeezed through a final pack of partiers and forced his elbow onto the bar, claiming a space next to his friend.

"Made it," he said, nearly shouting in order to be heard. "Did you get me a beer?"

"It's probably warm by now," Harry answered, sliding over a full glass of beer. "Jammed, huh."

David looked about and nodded, acknowledging the obvious. He swallowed a large portion of the beer.

"Tough saving me a seat, though, I guess."

"I had to give it up, David. There were too many women willing to rub up against my thighs for a stool. What took you so long? It's not like you have a job that kept you."

"Don't start, Harry. I work. I have a job."

"Some job. You can work when you want; stay in your pajamas all day. You should experience some real business problems. That would force you to grow up."

David sensed the source of his friend's animosity. "Trouble at the cookie factory, then?"

Harry drained the beer from his glass and pushed it to the far edge of the bar. "Your round," he pointed out before responding to David's question. "Yep. I've been doing battle with Mr. Walter Whalen again today. It's very frustrating."

"Who's Walter Whalen?"

"Walter Whalen is the big deal owner of six Super Saver Marts. I've been trying for months to get our cookies into his stores, and he keeps putting me off. Two more," Harry interrupted his lament to deal with the bartender, who had picked up the empty beer mug. "Anyway," he turned his attention back to David, "today I invited him to go golfing at Oak Hills, figuring we could strike a deal on the course, and you know what he said?"

"No."

"He prefers tennis."

"So? You play tennis. Oak Hills has good courts. Invite him to play tennis."

"I tried, but he just brushed me off. It's very disheartening."

Seeking some heartening conversation, David changed the subject. "So, are you ready for Larry's wedding? We should be able to have some fun up in Wisconsin tomorrow."

"More than ready. I bought a new shirt and tie and even got a haircut. Which you could use, you know." Harry glanced deprecatingly at his friend's long hair, pulled back in a ponytail.

Long accustomed to it, David responded to his friend's familiar criticism with an indulgent smile.

The bartender returned with two more beers, and David paid him, but held on to his original, unfinished drink.

"You're not bringing a date to the wedding, are you?" Harry asked.

"A date? No. No date."

"Great, because," Harry leaned conspiratorially close, "Lar says about a dozen of his bride's unmarried sorority sisters are going to be there. And some cousins and high school friends. We're bound to be able to find someone ... hey, that's right," suddenly recalling another avenue of attack, Harry warmed to further sarcasm. "It's just about that time of year again, isn't it?"

"You're starting, Harry."

"No, really. Summer's approaching; the season for another of your great romances, like 'What's her name' from last summer and the nurse the year before. I figure it must have something to do with Vietnam. You can only have sex during hot weather now."

"You're an idiot, Harry. Surely we have something better to do than conduct a seasonal analysis of my dating habits."

"We do." Harry drank a large portion of his beer. "We can finish these and have another."

"Not me, thanks." David emptied his first glass and shoved the second in front of his friend. "Have mine. I'm off. I'll see you tomorrow at the wedding."

"Wait," Harry protested, "don't go. You just got here. Look at all the women. We can't help but find someone to go home with."

"Good plan, Harry, but I want to get a run in, then take it easy tonight. Get to bed early. We've got a long drive north tomorrow and are likely to do some heavy drinking. And eating."

"You take this exercise stuff too seriously, David," he admonished. "You're too skinny. You need some healthy beer flab."

"You may be right. I'll see you at the church tomorrow."

"And get a haircut," Harry tossed after his departing friend, who, making his way back to the door, was quickly lost from sight as the milling crowd closed behind him.

Having forced his way to the door and through it, David paused in the welcome calm of the sidewalk, breathing deeply of the clear May air that hinted of warmer evenings to come. Though nearly a dozen miles from downtown Chicago, the suburban street on which the bar was located was on relatively high ground, and in the distance David could see the brightly lit upper portion of the still new, in 1971, John Hancock Building.

A couple, walking along the sidewalk happily wrapped in each other's arms, distracted his attention from the city skyline. He watched them approach the tavern and, though initially daunted by the pack of bodies just inside, determinedly push their way inside. When the door had shut behind them, David strode off in the direction from which they had come.

After a walk of several blocks, he reached his parked car, and a short drive brought him home to a cluster of unremarkable two-story suburban apartment buildings, one of which contained his own apartment. Having parked in his customary spot at the tree-lined far edge of the parking lot, he quickly conducted a habitual scan of the parking area to confirm that there were no neighbors to observe him and connect him with his vehicle. Satisfied that he would be unnoticed, he walked swiftly to his building, entered the lobby, and climbed the flight of stairs to the bland hallway in which one door, identical to all the others save for the number on the small brass plate, was his.

Once inside his own home, he walked the length of a narrow hallway, at the end of which was a full-length mirror, to his bedroom where he pulled off his clothes, tossing them into the corner of a closet extending the entire length of one wall. From the mass of clean and dirty clothing inextricably mixed on the closet floor, he grabbed some sweat clothes and a pair of running shoes. He suited up, did some stretching, then went outside and, in the gentling evening light, took a four-mile run that ended back in the parking lot.

Home once more, trailing discarded, sweaty clothing behind, he hurried along the hallway to the bathroom where he drew a hot bath and gently eased himself into the water. He lay still, soaking for a few minutes, then washed himself thoroughly and, taking a razor from the edge of the tub, began to shave. He worked slowly and carefully on the sparse stubble spotting his legs, but the rest of his body required only a few quick strokes to be completely smooth.

David slid his hands approvingly over his hairless body, then pulled the plug and stepped out of the tub. Standing at the vanity mirror, he meticulously shaved his face, working until satisfied that no hair could be felt. Reaching behind his neck, he freed his long hair from the rubber band that held it in a tight ponytail and shook it loose about his shoulders.

He wrapped a large towel around his body, tucking it just under his arms, and on the way to the bedroom paused in front of the full-length mirror to study the appearance of his legs, exposed beneath the towel. Pleased, he went on to the bedroom, dropped the towel, and, leaning into the closet, pushed the hanging clothes aside to expose a narrow wall locker that he opened using a key retrieved from a hook hidden just inside the closet door.

With a satisfied smile at the revealed assortment of dresses, skirts, and blouses hanging within the locker, he removed a cardboard box from the shelf above them, carried it to his bed and withdrew from it a pair of black lace trimmed women's underpants. Stepping into them produced a rush of physical pleasure that heightened when he slipped his arms through the straps of a matching brassiere and reached behind his back to secure the hooks. He next extracted from the box a pair of silicone breast forms and settled one into each of the cups of the bra, adjusting them until they felt as correctly positioned and natural as possible.

He closed his eyes and, embracing a consuming sensation of relief and comfort brought on by the feel and smell of the clothing, surrendered David to the ascension of Lynn.

A glance at the clock on the dresser cut short Lynn's appreciation of her release. Focusing again on dressing, she took from the box a black garter belt and a pair of stockings. Sitting on the edge of her bed, she carefully and pleasurably drew first one stocking, then the other, each over an artfully posed leg, pulling them up to her thighs and securing them with the straps of the garter belt.

With the stockings in place, Lynn rose and reached once more into the box, taking out a black slip, which she dropped over her upraised arms and tantalizingly eased down her body. She lay back on the bed and moved her hips about to feel the silken slip against her smooth skin. Unfortunately, another check of the clock forced her to rise, return to the cabinet, and take a second box from the shelf. She dumped this box' contents, a supply of cosmetics, onto the dresser and working swiftly with a careful and experienced hand, applied the makeup, striving to achieve a subtle, understated feminine effect, a goal made more attainable by a fortuitously youthful face. After a final touch of eyeliner and lipstick, she gently brushed her shoulder length hair into a luxuriously feminine style.

Satisfied with the result reflected in the dresser mirror, she went to the kitchen and prepared a small salad, which she carried, walking with an accomplished, graceful stride, to the living room where she turned on the television and sat on the sofa to eat, paying more attention to her posture than to the television.

She ate quickly, glancing repeatedly at herself, shifting about on the sofa to enjoy the feel of her clothing. Gradually, as she was able to sink more deeply into femininity, David slipped farther into the background. Lynn frequently tilted her head to allow her hair to play about her shoulders and face. She began to see her legs as a woman's legs, her identity as truly female, and by the time the sun had completely set, most vestiges of maleness had also faded. She rose from the sofa and, watching her reflection in the darkened sliding glass door to the apartment's balcony, turned off the television and returned to the bedroom.

From the clothing arrayed in the cabinet, she selected a soft, flowing peasant blouse and a tight, black skirt. She savored the act of dressing, of stepping into the skirt and of watching the blouse take shape over her breasts as she allowed it to gently settle over her head and drop below her waist. Finally, with a culminating thrill of sensual pleasure, she stepped into a pair of high-heeled shoes.

She walked around the bedroom, practicing the rhythm of a woman's sensual walk, then grabbed a purse from the cabinet shelf and stuffed it with the cosmetics, some money, and David's driver's license, this last hidden deeply within an interior pocket. A final check in the full-length hallway mirror proved reassuring, and Lynn partially opened her apartment door, pausing to listen for movement in the outer hallway. Hearing no one, she stepped out and walked to the building's lobby, angry with herself for having hesitated. Her caution had been the act of her male identity; she had not been a woman, but rather a man worried about being seen dressed in woman's clothing.

Crossing the parking lot to her car, Lynn listened to the sound of her heels on the pavement, concentrated on the feel of the tight skirt pulling against her thighs and once more loosening the grip of masculinity. Unexpectedly, her pathway approached a man who had apparently just parked his car and was walking toward her, and without reasonable strategy for evading the encounter, she returned his smile and continued swiftly on, grateful for her policy of avoiding as much as possible her fellow residents and for the fact that she had never before encountered this man, that he could not connect her automobile with David. Reaching her car, she glanced back and discovered that he too was looking back, though thankfully not altering his direction. She opened the car door and stepped into the driver's seat in a manner that caused her skirt to rise to mid-thigh. A surreptitious check confirmed that the man had paused to watch, and Lynn felt the joy she assumed all women feel when the objects of appreciative attention.

She drove out of the parking lot, turned north, and passed through quiet residential neighborhoods. A few blocks from her home she was forced to stop for a traffic signal and while waiting for the light to change, she glanced at a car that had pulled up on her right. The driver was a woman, and inadvertently, David was attracted by her beauty.

The light turned green and the woman drove off, quickly pulling ahead and leaving Lynn disgusted with herself.

"I'm a woman," she harshly reminded herself, "and not a lesbian. Get it right."

Again she had to work to assert her identity. Her car's standard transmission afforded frequent opportunity to consciously experience driving in a skirt and high-heeled shoes, and Lynn gradually returned.

She turned east on a major thoroughfare and drove up an entrance ramp to the northbound Tri-State Tollway. From the elevated roadway the storied Chicago skyline was clearly visible to the east, and Lynn enjoyed an occasional glance at its luster until approach to a tollbooth required her attention. She slowed her car into one of the attendant-manned lanes, and the less than subtle appraisal of her legs the tolltaker permitted himself as he took Lynn's dollar and returned her change considerably aided her journey into femininity.

Twenty minutes later she pulled the car onto an exit ramp, left the tollway, and drove several miles east through one of the northwestern suburbs, eventually turning into the parking lot of a small, dark, and undistinguished strip mall. Driving slowly past the closed shops, she paid particular attention to an unlit door marked only by the painted designation "Charlie's," and found a parking spot several storefronts beyond.

Lynn took advantage of the act of exiting her car to once more appreciate how her skirt displayed credibly female legs. On the sidewalk that ran the length of the string of stores, she paused in front of a darkened shop window to check her appearance, straighten her skirt and tousle her hair. Satisfied, she turned and began her walk back to "Charlie's," passing closed, nondescript businesses that seemed incapable of attracting interest, even when open. She wondered who would shop there and reflected that at night there were probably more cars in the parking lot than there would be during business hours.

Walking quickly, she glanced at herself in each successive window and the sight and sound of her walk filled her thoroughly with Lynn.

She pulled open the clouded glass door beneath the painted sign, entering a small vestibule, then opened a second door and walked into the soft neon glow of a long, narrow, low-ceilinged tavern.

"Well, Hello, Lynn," chimed the bartender, who was rather idly watching the door from a stool behind the bar.

2.

"Hi, Barry," Lynn answered, pausing just inside the door, allowing her eyes to adjust to the dimly lit tavern.

A few patrons were scattered about the horseshoe shaped bar that stretched from just left of the entrance about a third of the way into the room, then curved around to end against the same front wall. Others, alone or in pairs, sat at tables placed on raised platforms along the left and right walls beyond the bar. In the center, not far from the farthest reach of the bar, was a pool table, prominent beneath the establishment's only bright light. Beyond that a wooden dance floor occupied most of the remaining space, extending to the back wall, much of which was covered with a huge mirror.

"Quiet here, tonight," Lynn observed.

"You're just early, hon," Barry countered. "Vodka and 7-UP?"

Lynn smiled and nodded affirmatively. She had, upon entering "Charlie's," briefly become the focus of attention, and she was pleased that several men had watched her as she strode confidently around the bar to a place on the far side. As she settled onto a barstool, Barry arrived with her drink.

"You look great tonight, Hon," he offered as he placed the glass onto a coaster. "Love your outfit."

"Thanks, Barry. I appreciate that," Lynn responded, placing some bills on the bar. When Barry had collected what he needed and gone to the cash register for her change, she more thoroughly surveyed the room, studying the people drawn together by the unique appeal of "Charlie's." She offered a quick and shallow smile to a man seated a few stools away and making no effort to conceal his inspection of her. Other unaccompanied men, sitting at the bar or at one of the several tables lining the tavern's walls, exhibited vacant expressions born of caution, of wishing to invite no attention.

Barry soon returned and, as the few early evening customers were not keeping him busy, dragged a stool to a spot across the bar from Lynn.

"Friday night, Barry," Lynn observed. "Early or late, there aren't many people here for a Friday night. Have you been offending the customers?"

The bartender looked about the room. "It is a bit slow," he conceded, "but give it another hour; the girls will be coming – no pun intended." Barry laid a hand on Lynn's arm and chuckled at his joke. "Are you meeting Randy?"

"Yes, at least I hope so. I want to get a long evening in. It's going to be the last for a while."

"Going away?" Barry inquired, leaning close across the bar.

"No. It's just that summer's almost here, and I won't be able to shave my body anymore, so this is it until next fall. I trust you'll still be here then."

"Well, Sugar," Barry struck a pose of exaggerated seriousness, "as always, I plan to move on to bigger and better things, but 'Charlie's' will always be here. As will I, most likely."

A rush of fresh air indicated the opening of the tavern door, and, as did the rest of the patrons, Barry and Lynn turned to see who had entered. Several women, or ostensibly women, some more convincingly female than others, walked in from the vestibule and, becoming the center of attention as had Lynn in her turn, paused just inside the entrance. One of the girls, as her eyes adjusted to the dim lighting, recognized Lynn, waved, and detached herself from her companions as they moved on to the tables in the back.

Barry excused himself. "Duty calls, Hon," he said as he left, lifting a section of the bar's surface and passing beneath it to serve the new arrivals.

Lynn turned on her stool to take the hand of the girl who had come around the bar to speak with her.

"Jeannie, you look wonderful," Lynn said as she held her friend at arm's length and appreciatively studied her.

Jeannie's low cut dress offered assurance that her breasts, though small, were real, and Lynn noticed other, more subtle changes: an undeniably feminine curve at her waist, a greater fullness of her hips, and a vaguely perceptible softness of spirit.

Shadowing Lynn's study, Jeannie looked down at her own breasts.

"Nearly a year now," she reported. "The hormones are doing their work. I'm wildly pleased. About another year, I think, 'till the operation."

"That's ... a bit scary." Lynn struggled with the concept. "How have you handled this at work?"

"I had to get a new job. Actually, I've pretty well got a new life, haven't I? And I love it."

"Well, I'm certainly happy for you. I'm afraid I find the thought more than a bit frightening. I'm not certain I would want to be an old lady."

"The alternative is to have never been a young lady." Jeannie stepped closer. "You think you'd never do it, but wait. As the years pass, the urge grows stronger. You'll see. The need will take over, particularly as you begin to see the opportunity slipping away. I turned thirty this year, and had to consider how difficult it would be to begin as a woman at forty or fifty. I didn't want to lose all the young years. It hasn't been a casual decision." She leaned over and kissed Lynn on the cheek. "But enough of that. I have to join my friends. Stop by the table later." She turned to leave, but hesitated and fumbled about in her purse. "I have something for you," she said, extracting a business card and handing it to Lynn. "Here. It's the therapist who starts it all."

Lynn attempted to hand the card back, but Jeannie drew away.

"Hang on to it," she advised. "She's just the first step. One day you may find you want to call her. Just don't wait so long that you're too old and living with the bitterness of having missed out. We get only one go-around."

Left alone, Lynn grew a bit morose. She studied the card briefly, then, turning back to the bar, tossed it into a nearby ashtray. Shifting her posture to assume a more feminine pose, she looked down at her bodice, a disguise, really, she resignedly admitted to herself. It struck her then that it was just that preoccupation with herself that Randy had interrupted the night they met. Looking about the tavern, she also realized that she had been sitting in the very same spot, or certainly almost exactly the same, when he first approached her.

Her self-assessment that fall evening when she was still a rather new patron of "Charlie's" was cut short by the abrupt plop of a beer mug onto the bar beside her own drink. Gripping the mug and settling onto the stool beside her was a tall, pleasant-looking, Lynn thought, if not exactly handsome, though undeniably muscular and no doubt athletic, man.

"I saw you checking yourself out," he said, smiling. "No need. You look great. In fact, until you did that, I had thought you might be a real woman; you're that good."

Lynn disgustedly twirled her stool away from her admirer.

"Hostility?" he questioned. "Why? It was a sincere compliment."

Lynn looked over her shoulder. "If you understood 'Charlie's,'" she rather coldly answered, "and the girls here, understood me, you would realize that I'm here to be a woman, not to be reminded that I'm not... a woman."

"Ah," the man relaxed against the back of the stool, "I see. But actually, I do understand 'Charlie's' and you, or sort of you. What you mean, anyway. I'm something of a veteran here."

"I've never seen you." Attempting to convey disinterest, Lynn took a sip from her drink.

"Well, it has been a while since I've been in, but the fact that you haven't seen me doesn't mean I haven't been here. I've never seen you here either; perhaps I should question your authority to speak for 'Charlie's' girls."

Lynn remained aloof, pushing her empty glass to the inside of the bar to attract Barry's attention.

"Please," the man finished his beer and again placed his glass beside Lynn's, "let me buy this round as an attempt to seek forgiveness. I am sorry I offended."

Offered no indication of a thaw, he took another tack. "Barry," he called out, lending some credibility to his claim to be a regular customer. He alerted the bartender to the two empty glasses, then addressed Lynn. "Would you like to dance? Barry will have our drinks here by the time we get back.

Lynn looked across the room to the dance floor where two couples were gyrating to "The Rolling Stones."

"I'm not really much of a dancer," she confessed, softening her resistance to the man's approach. "If there were a slow song…"

"Say no more," the man offered brightly.

He hopped off of his stool with an athleticism that confirmed Lynn's initial impression. She watched him stride quickly through the tavern to the very back wall where, from an elevated booth, a disk jockey was playing records and she continued to observe him as he strode purposefully back following a short consultation with the DJ.

"It's done," he announced, and as he offered to take Lynn's hand, the more romantic sound of "Unchained Melody" by "The Righteous Brothers" supplanted Mick Jagger.

Her fortress breached, unable, and really, not desiring to resist further, Lynn took Randy's hand and stepped down from her stool.

Though momentarily frustrated when she hesitated before extending the correct hand, Lynn was quickly enthralled as her partner pulled her close, wrapping his arm around her waist. That she could feel that he could feel her breasts against his chest was exciting.

"My name is Randy," he said, leaning back a bit to look into Lynn's eyes.

About to offer her own name in response, Lynn held fire, distracted when she realized that her right hand, entwined with Randy's left, distinctly felt a ring. She looked at their hands, turning them so she could see his ring finger.

"Yes," Randy confidently maintained his smile, "I am married, but my wife and I have differing views on some matters."

"What mat…"

Lynn's inquiry was stifled in its infancy when Randy, lifting his right hand from her waist, pressed her head onto his shoulder and held her more closely. She made a feeble physical protest, but allowed herself to be drawn into the sensual pleasure of the dance.

Randy held Lynn a moment beyond the last notes of the music, then released her and, taking her hand, led her back to the bar where, as he had predicted, two more drinks awaited.

"That was wonderful. Thank you," Lynn said with a touch of sadness that the dance had ended. The lingering pleasure of her experience, though, invited closer approach by her new acquaintance; left discovery of his marital status in a deeply unobtrusive background.

They talked together for more than an hour, discovered mutual interests in tennis and exercise. They danced again on those few occasions when the music selection permitted, and as the hour approached closing time, Randy addressed the question of continuing their relationship outside of the tavern.

"I don't see how we can," Lynn regretfully suggested, the impediment of Randy's marriage resurfacing. "I have no interest in being the 'other woman.'"

"You aren't," Randy replied.

"Not funny. Actually, that's cold. I told you before..."

"Yes," Randy interrupted, "but it's true. It is, in fact, the point. As you have no wish to be the other woman injuring a marriage, I have no intention of breaking my marriage vows by betraying my wife with another woman."

Lynn frowned, turned again away from Randy, and attempted to reconcile with her moral dilemma her interest in the man and her undeniable arousal.

"How do you get away with this?" she asked. "Doesn't your wife wonder what you're doing?"

"I've pulled it off so far," Randy answered. "I travel a lot for work…"

"What do you do?" Lynn interrupted.

"I'm a management consultant, and…"

"Management consultant?" she interrupted again, suppressing a chuckle. "You're kidding." She placed an appreciative hand on one of his biceps. "As built as you are, I would have gone with construction worker."

"I work out a lot. Anyway," Randy expressed some frustration, "If you'd let me finish. I travel frequently and can sometimes get back earlier than my itinerary calls for. If I've driven, I have transportation. If I've flown, then I rent a car, drive back to the airport the next day, and get picked up off the originally scheduled flight. Either way, I can spend an evening here." Randy took Lynn's hand. "I mentioned that I had been coming to 'Charlie's' for a while. I used to spend evenings with one of the girls here, and this system worked well. She's gone now, but we had a great relationship. It was positive for both of us and caused no difficulties for anyone."

He paused, and though Lynn made no response, she crossed her legs in a manner she hoped suggestive and looked at her suitor with expectation, inviting further explanation.

Encouraged, Randy began again. "We met when we could, no entanglements, just mutual pleasure." He paused again and though offered no indication of acceptance, neither was he rejected.

"She was submissive," he announced.

Lynn pulled her hand back.

"What do you mean? You smacked her around?" She withdrew as far as the stool allowed.

"No. No, nothing like that."

"What, then? You tied her up?"

"Yes, that was pretty much it. You remember I said my wife and I differ on some matters; well, that's something in which she has no interest, but I enjoy it, and so did my friend."

Lynn faced the bar and consumed the remainder of her Vodka and 7-Up. Randy waited.

"This is a bit much," Lynn finally offered. I'm stunned. I had hoped we could spend some time tonight."

"We can. I have a place."

"A place is not the problem, Randy. I have no interest in experiencing pain."

"Nor have I any interest in inflicting it. There's no pain; only pleasure. Actually, my friend used to tell me that nothing made her feel as much a woman as being tied up. It is, after all, rather primal."

Randy tossed some bills onto the bar and got up from his stool, his tone becoming somewhat matter-of-fact. "Listen, Lynn," he said, "it's just about closing time. I have to hit the bathroom. Tell Barry, please," he indicated the money, "that it's all his, and then I hope you'll decide to go out with me. We don't have to do anything you're not comfortable with."

Lynn watched him make his way to the back of the tavern and when he had disappeared into the hall containing the bathrooms, she frantically signaled for her bartender friend.

"Barry," she whispered intensely, leaning over the bar when he arrived. "Oh, yes," she noticed the bartender's glance at the money Randy had left, "that's for you. Keep it. We're done. But listen, that guy wants to tie me up."

"I thought he might. Who wouldn't?"

"It's not funny, Barry. I'm really attracted to him, but - Wait! You know about this?"

"Sure. He spent time with one of the girls here, Margie. She was really nice."

"Was? What, did he kill her?"

Barry laughed, scooped up the money, and grabbed the empty glasses. "No," he explained, "Margie decided to completely transition. She moved to New York City for a clean start, but she had been a regular here. Randy and she were a steady thing. There was never any trouble. He's safe."

"Safe? You're sure? This Margie discussed it with you?"

"Not the intimate details, certainly, and had she shared them, they would be sacrosanct. What happens in 'Charlie's' or outside 'Charlie's' stays zipped. A bartender's code. But I can assure you that Randy and Margie had a mutually pleasurable relationship."

"Painless?"

"My understanding is that they enjoyed mild bondage, no SM or hardcore. Once they came to a Halloween party here as a Viking and his chained Greek captive. Pretty cool."

"But I've never done anything like this."

"Then give it a shot. Lynn, I know Randy never forced Margie into anything she didn't want to do, and that's more than can be said for many relationships." Barry directed Lynn's attention to the brightened bar lights and the flow of departing patrons. "I've got to get on with closing. My advice is to give it a chance. I'll see you next week."

"I hope so," she mumbled to herself as Barry departed.

Lynn's reminiscence, however, was prevented from progressing through the rest of her first night with Randy. It was interrupted, just as had happened the evening she was reliving, by the thump of a beer mug placed beside her glass. The quick surmise that Randy had arrived was just as quickly dispelled when an arm wrapped around her shoulders and a body pressed against her side. Looking over her shoulder, she discovered herself to be the object of an unfamiliar and obviously inebriated man's leering attention.

"Hey, Honey," he said as Lynn attempted to lean away. "I saw you checking yourself out, and thought I should too." He looked her over intently. "You're good. Great legs."

"Listen…" leaning still farther away from the man, Lynn attempted to curtail his approach, but, oblivious, he paid no attention.

"I'm glad to see you're not with the other girls," he continued as, with the hand not about her shoulders, he pulled Lynn's skirt up a few inches.

Lynn pushed his hand from her leg and pulled the skirt back toward her knees, but not before the man had achieved his goal.

"You're wearing a garter belt and stockings. I love that. Mind if I join you?"

Without waiting for an answer, he sat on the vacant stool beside Lynn, keeping his hand on her back.

"I enjoy talking to women as pretty as you are. You have a great shape. I bet you're a good looking guy, too."

Lynn twisted on her seat to escape his attempt to rub her thigh and removed his hand from her shoulder.

"Don't put your hands on me," she demanded.

"O. K., O. K., don't get all huffy."

He moved a bit away, but, ultimately undaunted, continued his pursuit.

"So, what do you like to do, then?" he asked.

"Like to do?"

"Yeah, you know. For fun."

"Well, I like to play tennis," Lynn offered.

"No, no," the man grew exasperated. "Jeez, are you going to be difficult? I mean, what do you like to do?" He emphasized the last word with a particularly salacious grin. "What kind of... Whoa! Wait a minute!"

His attention had suddenly leaped to the other side of the bar where a woman just entering the tavern had paused, more to be checked out by those in the room than to check them out. Tall and slim, she possessed strikingly blond hair that cascaded below her shoulders and was wearing a skin-tight, startlingly low-cut dress from which enormous breasts threatened to escape at any moment. Several other girls of somewhat less dramatic aspect trailed in behind her.

Lynn's intruder muttered a perfunctory, "Excuse me," and frantically made his way around the bar to join a cluster of people exchanging kisses and embraces with the newcomer.

Keeping an eye on the scene at the door, Barry appeared in front of Lynn and picked up her empty glass.

"Another?" he asked. "Your friend certainly departed abruptly."

"Oh, please," Lynn jokingly pleaded. "That," she indicated the exuberant group the interloper had joined, "was a fortuitous arrival. It certainly rescued me."

"Yes," Barry observed, "Miss Marilyn has made her signature *veni, vidi, vici* entrance. I'm glad it served some good purpose for once." He leaned conspiratorially close. "It's amazing what some silicone can do, isn't it?"

"Don't be catty, Barry."

"Catty?" Barry recoiled in mock horror. "I'm never catty. You've hurt me, cut me to the quick, as they say. I may water your drink," he threatened as he went to get Lynn another Vodka and 7UP.

The tall blond, triumphantly leading her entourage, slowly and flamboyantly made her way to the rear of the room and joined, or rather assumed command of, the women seated at the tables there. Lynn's leering man had joined Miss Marilyn's camp followers, and Lynn, freed from his importunities and with the new and presumably undiluted drink Barry had brought, settled back to quietly enjoy, while awaiting Randy's arrival, the evolving spectacle of shifting romances and intrigues.

She occasionally watched her reflection in a mirror hung on the far wall, across the bar, and played with her hair in what she felt to be a particularly girlish manner, but the inebriated man's allusion to her true gender had compromised her illusion, leaving her feeling like a man in a dress. A trip to the ladies' room to freshen her makeup, she thought, would help. If nothing else, it would afford an opportunity to walk across the wooden dance floor in high heels.

She stepped gracefully from the barstool, secured her purse, and walked resolutely away from the bar, past the pool table, and onto the vacant dance floor. Listening to the sound of her heels on the wooden surface, feeling again the tightness of her skirt, and watching herself in the mirrored back wall, she felt Lynn returning. She looked good, she thought, and certainly her clothing felt wonderful.

In front of the ladies' room mirror she applied some lipstick, taking reassurance from that particularly feminine ritual. She brushed her hair, pleased by the shape her breasts imparted to her blouse as she raised her arms.

Leaving the bathroom some minutes later with a considerably revived confidence, she felt no compulsion to monitor her reflection as she recrossed the dance floor and resumed her seat, though the inadvertent rise of her skirt and subsequent view of her legs as she climbed onto the stool were greatly reassuring.

"Charlie's" became more crowded as the evening advanced. The bar and the tables filled, the disk jockey came on duty and began playing music, and the dance floor soon overflowed. Groups gathered to play a mechanical darts game at the wall behind Lynn, and couples waited their turns at the pool table, stacking quarters on the table's edge to reserve their spots.

Lynn nursed her drink for a while, then suddenly drained it and ordered another when the harried Barry briefly became available. She amused herself by watching the swirl of convoluted sexual politics surrounding her until the appearance, just inside the door, of an athletically trim man, a man tall enough to be seen above the mass of clustered bodies that obscured and rendered unnoticeable most arrivals, particularly animated her. She rose up on the barstool, waving energetically as he paused to look about. When his searching gaze discovered Lynn, he returned her greeting and plunged into the crowd to make his way through to her. Lynn anxiously traced his progress around the bar and when he was able to squeeze in beside her, she eagerly responded to his kiss.

"Randy," she said with obvious joy, "I'm so glad you made it. Do you have all night?"

"All night. My flight's due in tomorrow evening, so we've plenty of time."

Randy hopped onto the stool so recently vacated by Lynn's unwelcome and fickle admirer and raised his hand to apprise Barry of his arrival and need for a beer. When he turned again to face Lynn, she pushed her knees between his and leaned close to whisper, but the sudden arrival of the bartender, delivering a beer, interrupted.

"Randy," Barry said, grasping the newcomer's hand, "I see you've found the lady."

"Sure have," Randy answered. "How are you tonight? It looks like you're busy."

"You shouldn't ask. It would take too long. Just look at this crowd. I'm overworked, underpaid, and under-appreciated."

"Barry, bring another of what the lady's drinking, and I'll appreciate you."

After some discussion of Randy's business trip, Lynn announced her own schedule. "I can stay the night, but I have to be off early in the morning. I'm going to a wedding up in Wisconsin."

"Yours?"

"Mine?" Lynn failed to understand.

"Your wedding?"

"You two are getting married?" Barry reappeared, placing Lynn's drink on the bar. "I'm simply thrilled. Tell me I'm the first to know."

"You would indeed be the first, Barry," Lynn reached for her fresh drink. "Go serve some customers who may tip you."

Feigning disappointment, Barry counted out some bills from those Randy had placed on the bar. "Ah, well," he sighed, "you'd have made a beautiful bride."

When Barry had once again departed, Lynn leaned close to Randy, placing an arm around his shoulders.

"No," she spoke softly, "It's not my wedding. It's a college friend of David's. I'm really sorry, but I do have to go. Actually, I really want to. It just means I'll have to leave early."

"We'll live with it." Randy touched her cheek. "It's just unfortunate timing, but we've experienced that before. We'll have all night, and other nights."

Lynn looked abruptly away from her lover, focusing on the bar, but Randy grasped her chin and turned her head back.

"Listen," he slipped a hand between her legs until his fingers reached just beneath the hem of her skirt, "I have something new for tonight."

"Have you?" Lynn took his other hand in both of hers and leaned forward to give him a kiss. "What is it?"

Randy smiled, then drank from his glass of beer. "You'll just have to wait. It's a surprise."

The two sat together talking of commonplace things — politics, sports, music — until Barry interrupted them to point out that the man who had earlier accosted Lynn was heading out the door in the company of Miss Marilyn.

"I guess he found something to do, then," Lynn said. In response to Randy's puzzled look, she again wrapped an arm around his shoulders. "It's just something that guy said to me earlier. It doesn't matter."

Just then some completely unexpected music caught her attention. "Randy," she said, "it's a slow song. The DJ has actually played a slow song." She looked pleadingly into Randy's eyes. "Let's dance. We could dance to this and then go."

"My pleasure." Randy held out an inviting hand to Lynn and led her to the dance floor where they found some space among other couples, some exclusively male and others, like themselves, apparently composed of male and female.

Lynn pressed her body against Randy, as much for herself to feel her breasts as for her partner to enjoy them. Avoiding taking the lead initially required some attention, but as they danced, she felt more deeply immersed in femininity. She became a woman dancing in a man's arms, stepping quickly in high heels when they turned, and growing increasingly excited when Randy pushed a leg between hers, tightening her skirt.

When the song ended, Lynn stood for a moment to compose herself and while holding Randy by the hand to keep him from starting back to the bar, she noticed Jeannie, seated at a table along the wall, give her a rather impish wave and with it an opportunity for calming conversation.

"See that girl waving? The one in the low-cut red dress." Lynn directed Randy's attention as she returned Jeannie's wave. "Her name's Jeannie."

"Yes?" Randy also offered a small wave.

"She was sort of my voice coach when I started coming here."

"Voice coach?"

"Yes," Lynn explained. "She helped me learn to sound at least reasonably feminine when speaking. Anyway, those breasts are her own. She grew them." Sufficiently collected, Lynn began to move off the dance floor. "And," she continued, "she and I had an interesting conversation earlier."

"Interesting in what way?"

The two regained their seats at the bar, and, after a sip of her drink, Lynn continued her story. "She's having the surgery."

"That's nice."

"She says I'll want to have it."

"Will you?"

"How would you feel if I did?"

Randy hesitated, then smiled. "Well, I couldn't convince myself that I wasn't actually cheating on my wife with another woman."

"Is that what ended your relationship with Margie?"

"What? Her surgery?"

Lynn nodded.

"Sort of." Randy pondered. "Actually, looking back, I didn't have to give her change much consideration; her move to New York pretty well finished our time together."

Though Lynn actively pursued the conversation no further, she quietly considered it, a silence upon which, for a few moments, Randy did not intrude. When he had consumed the last of his beer, though, he placed a gentle hand on Lynn's lap.

"Are you ready to go?" he asked.

Brightening, Lynn looked up. "I am." She finished her drink and collected her purse.

Barry, seeing them prepare to leave, came over to bid them goodnight. "Leaving, then?" he asked, gathering up his tip and the empty glasses. "Lynn, I'll see you next…"

Lynn's eyes grew large, and her expression conveyed dismay. She shook her head almost imperceptibly, hoping Randy wouldn't notice.

"...time," Barry finished.

Lynn smiled with relief. "Next time," she echoed.

Grasping Randy's arm, she began walking with him through the crowd, but suddenly stopped.

"Wait a minute," she said, releasing Randy and making her way back to the bar where two men had already occupied the stools she and Randy had abandoned. Excusing herself, she reached between the two and pulled from the ashtray in front of them the card Jeannie had given her. She shook off the ashes that had fallen on top of it and, after a sheepish smile for the two quizzical men, stuffed the card into her purse and rejoined Randy. Once again securing his arm, she walked with him out of the tavern and to her car.

"Same place?" she asked as Randy held the driver's side door open for her.

"Yes," he answered, "just park around the back near the north corner. We go in the same door as last time."

Randy, as Lynn hoped he would, watched her legs as she drew them into her car. When she was settled into the driver's seat, he pushed the door shut, walked to his own car and drove out of the parking lot with Lynn following. They turned left at the first traffic light and drove north for a few miles to a large and apparently busy motel. Parking behind the building, Randy waited for Lynn to find a spot. He did not approach her car after she had parked, but rather waited beside his own and watched her walk to him. Lynn enjoyed knowing that he found the vision pleasurable.

They embraced, then walked together through one of the motel's back doors, and Randy held Lynn close as they navigated a deserted hallway until he stopped at the room he had rented and, unlocking the door, stepped aside to let her enter first.

The room was unremarkable, possessed of standard motel accommodations: a bathroom to the right just inside the door, a dresser, one chair, and a double bed. As Lynn placed her purse on the dresser, Randy put his arms around her and, brushing her hair aside, kissed her neck.

"So," he spoke softly, "now you're mine."

"Yes," Lynn answered as she submitted to his embrace, "I am."

Lowering his arms from Lynn's shoulders, Randy held her wrists and drew them behind her, taking hold of them with one hand. With his free hand he pulled open a dresser drawer and removed a length of soft rope with which he tied her wrists together.

Lynn struggled just enough to test the bonds, then walked around the bed so Randy could watch her walk with bound hands. Returning, she pressed her body against his.

"So where's your surprise?" she asked.

"Sit here," he instructed, leading Lynn to the edge of the bed. He knelt beside her and pulled from beneath the dust ruffle a pair of small dog collars connected by a short length of chain. With a finger in one of the collars, he dangled his surprise in the air.

"Pretty neat, huh? I made it myself." He fastened a collar around each of Lynn's ankles and hopped onto the bed beside her. "Now walk."

Lynn stood up, tested the chain and the short stride it allowed her, then walked with restricted steps about the room, pausing often to strain against the bonds and to strike poses that she felt to be exciting and, she hoped, arousing for Randy. She walked into the bathroom to look at herself, twisting to see her bound wrists. Returning to the bedroom, she discovered that Randy had laid out on the bed several longer pieces of rope. She hobbled about the room some more, under her lover's watchful gaze, until he got up, approached her, and taking her by one of her arms, led her back to the bed. He wound one of the ropes around her upper body, pinning her arms and accentuating her breasts, then eased her down onto the bed. After removing the collars, he tied her ankles together, wrapping the rope around her calves and tying the end just below her knees.

"Now see if you can get free," he said.

Lynn worked first on her wrists, then struggled against the ropes securing her arms. Lying back, she strained her legs as well as her arms against the restraints. She watched her skirt edge higher as she struggled. The sight of her long, tied legs and of the high-heeled shoes beneath her bound ankles excited her. She grew increasingly aroused by the feel and sight of being a bound, helpless woman. Soon Randy climbed onto the bed next to her and ran his hands up her thighs.

3.

A narrow beam of bright sunlight streaming into the room through a gap between the curtains warmed Lynn's face, awakening her. She moved to roll over, but discovered that she was unable to do so. As she grew more awake and aware, she recalled her surroundings; that her wrists were tied above her head and fastened to the top of the bed, her ankles, chained in the dog collars, tied to the foot of the bed, and that though she was wearing her slip, underwear, stockings and shoes, a soundly sleeping Randy lay naked beside her. For a few moments she allowed herself to savor the memory of the night's pleasures, but a glance at the clock beside the bed captured her surprised attention. She pushed her hips against Randy and called his name.

"Untie me," she urged, "it's late. We've overslept."

Randy groaned, stretched, looked at the clock, then sat up and reached down to free her ankles. Before untying her wrists, though, he lay on top of her and began kissing her.

"Stop," Lynn protested when she could avoid his lips. "I've got to go."

"It's early."

"It's not." Lynn succeeded in stifling his advances. "I really have to go. I have a long drive."

Randy reluctantly untied her wrists and rolled back to his side of the bed, allowing Lynn to collect her clothes and breast forms from the floor, her purse from the dresser, and to disappear into the bathroom where, working quickly, she washed her face and thoroughly shaved. Having dressed and reapplied makeup, she sat beside her still lethargic lover.

"Stay a bit longer," he urged, seizing one of her wrists.

"I would if I could. Honest." She freed her wrist and leaned over to kiss him. "Listen, Randy," she began with unaccustomed gravity, "last night was great. I've enjoyed these times over the months since we met more than anything, but I'm not going to be around for a while."

"What do you mean, 'a while?' Why not?" Randy sat up, shaking any drowsiness he had felt.

"Well," Lynn answered carefully, "summer's approaching. David does a lot of outdoor activities during the summer; he plays tennis, wears shorts a lot, so he can't shave his body. I'm afraid I kind of disappear. I'll be back in the fall, though. Probably late September or October; certainly by Halloween." Her lover's displeasure was obvious. "Randy," she touched his cheek, "I'm going to miss this. You've made me feel more feminine than I'd thought possible. I've become more me, and I'm going to miss being me more than I ever have before… in other summers."

Randy made no response.

"This is not easy." Lynn reached for some idea that would help. "When cool weather returns," she tried, "I'll be back at 'Charlie's.' Maybe between now and the fall you'll convince your wife to let you tie her up and you won't need me."

"Not likely," Randy rather sullenly replied.

"Well, it will be for only a few months." Lynn studied Randy's face, and seeing that he was not to be consoled, stood up.

"I've really got to go. Here's my half of the room rent." She pulled some money from her purse and dropped it on the bed, then moved to the door where she paused, looking back. "See you in the fall, Randy," she said, then stepped into the hallway and closed the door behind her.

Somewhat less confident in the bright daylight, Lynn walked swiftly to her car. Thoughts of the imminent change, of her own, if only temporary, demise made the ride home less pleasant than had been the previous evening's trip.

4.

Two hours later David was retracing Lynn's path along the northbound Tri-State Tollway, though with a quite different destination ahead. As he drove past the exit Lynn had taken the previous evening on her journey to "Charlie's," he glanced briefly to the east along the street on which, indistinguishable in the urban clutter, the familiar tavern stood, no doubt empty and quiet in the wake of its Friday night drama. That road behind him, he concentrated on the highway and the day ahead. A few hours later he was searching through a small Wisconsin town for the church where his friend was to be married.

Given Lynn's late departure from the motel, David was late arriving at the church, and the wedding had begun before he slipped into a rear pew. Devoting little attention to the ceremony, he concentrated on the bridesmaids, several of whom he found attractive. He studied how they moved and contemplated how it would feel to wear a formal gown and long gloves. Wonderful, he concluded. Eventually adopting Harry's enthusiasm, he looked forward to the reception. When the ceremony ended, he slipped back out onto the wide church steps to await Harry and their other college friends.

"Get lost?" Harry asked as he handed David a bag of birdseed.

"No," David answered, "just got a later start than I had intended."

"So all that going home early, running, and resting stuff was pointless."

"Not entirely pointless, Harry." Defensively changing the subject, David drew his friend on to a more intense interest. "You were right about the bridesmaids. They're all beautiful."

"I know, I know," Harry immediately warmed to the subject. "We should have some great opportunities tonight."

This speculation was interrupted when the two friends were joined by several other classmates, and elated greetings gave way to initial forays into reminiscence, which were in their turn interrupted by the emergence from the church of the bridal party. The joyful gathering of college friends, however, soon reconvened in the local country club's basement banquet room.

When the reception had progressed beyond dinner and the band had begun playing, couples filled the dance floor, and the parents of the bride and groom circulated among the dinner tables to greet seldom-seen relatives and friends. The collection of the groom's college friends, however, hovered around the bar consuming prodigious amounts of beer and recounting even more prodigious exaggerations of youthful adventures.

As Harry, momentarily holding the floor with the retelling of a particularly amusing - mostly to himself - account of ribald misadventure, approached the story's high point, he noticed that David was inattentive, staring intently across the room. Halting his tale, he followed his friend's gaze and discovered it to be focused on a bridesmaid who had paused halfway down the flight of steps from the floor above and was leaning on the railing, apparently searching for someone.

"Bad choice," he told David. "She's nice."

"Yeah. I can see that."

"No," Harry explained, "I mean she really is nice. She has repeatedly rejected my best fantasies."

"You know her?" David eagerly asked.

"Sure. Her name's Jenny Harris. She's one of Mrs. Lar's sorority sisters. She lives in the suburbs; not far from you, actually."

Having located the person she had been seeking, the girl waved and flashed a smile that beamed with a joy so natural that it completely enthralled the man of whose admiring observation she was so unaware. She resumed her descent of the staircase, walking with a calm gracefulness that was in perfect harmony with the quiet beauty of her face. David watched her until she reached the bottom of the stairs and disappeared into the milling crowd of wedding guests.

Harry, discovering that the conversation had moved on without him and had in fact progressed several years beyond his unfinished story, grabbed David's arm and led him away from the bar.

"You're right," he said as he guided his friend toward the crowded jumble of tables.

"I am?"

"Yes, David, old buddy," Harry asserted, "it's time we ceased living in the past and found some loose drawers to fall in love with for the present night. It is, after all, spring."

"Again with the seasons." David freed himself from Harry's grasp. "You go ahead. I'm going to get another beer." He displayed his empty glass.

"Fine." Harry disgustedly continued on. "I'll just have to come up with two on my own, then. But don't expect me to share."

David watched his friend set off on his quest through a crowd that had grown increasingly festive. The bride and groom had made their obligatory secret departure, and the band, having completed the required standard wedding reception repertoire, had begun playing covers of rock tunes to entice the younger and more hard core revelers to the dance floor. Through the milling bodies David observed Harry stop beside a table, lean over to talk with its occupants, then drop from sight, apparently joining the seated group.

With Harry gone and a refill of his drink secured, he decided to circulate among the guests and set off in a direction other than that taken by his friend. He wandered rather aimlessly about the room, occasionally pausing to observe the varied celebratory activities, carefully studying the many formal gowns and how the women wearing them moved.

Eventually returning to the bar to rejoin his classmates, all hopelessly lost in a past more hilarious than it was possible to have been, he was startled, as he approached them, to find Jenny Harris, the girl from the staircase, standing beside them, apparently otherwise unnoticed and waiting to be served. He hesitated, then nervously stepped next to her, placing his empty glass on the bar.

"Hello," he said with a decided lack of confidence.

"Hello," the bridesmaid answered with a smile that confirmed all he had imagined about her beauty and appeal.

"Could I buy this one?" he asked.

"They're free." She pointed out the obvious.

"That was supposed to be a sort of joke," he said, trying to appear a bit less awkward.

"Ah, I see. Well, then," she graciously rescued him with a perfectly executed formal curtsy, "I accept your offer. You may."

David was enchanted by her manner and voice as well as by her beauty.

"My name is David Stewart," he introduced himself, holding out his hand, "one of Lar's - Larry's friends from college."

"You're David Stewart?" Jenny seemed stunned.

David's surprise exceeded hers. "Yes, I am, but..." Flustered, he found no finish for his sentence.

"One of your friends was just telling me about you," she explained. "He told me all about your heroism in Vietnam. I'm certainly proud to meet you. My name is Jenny Harris."

"Harry."

"No, Harris."

"I meant the person who told you all this is Harry." David was exasperated.

"Yes, that's right. He tells me you had a rather horrific time. I'm awfully glad you made it home safely."

"Harry." David's awkwardness upon encountering Jenny was completely vanquished by annoyance. "Listen, Jenny, you have to understand. Harry's a nut. I imagine he made up everything he said. He probably thought he was helping me."

"Helping you?"

David realized his error. "Ah. Well. Yes. I had sort of noticed you earlier, and I guess he was pumping me up. He means well. He's just very creative."

"I see." Jenny saw more than David had intended. "Then you weren't in Vietnam?"

"Actually," David tried to rally, "I was. That much is true. I was there. A grunt." His stumbling both responded to and exacerbated

Jenny's obvious confusion. "Infantry. Okay, here it is. I was there, but I really didn't do much of anything out of the ordinary. Ordinary for there. I guess that really isn't ordinary. I mean, Harry was embellishing. He always embellishes. He's ..."

"An embellisher?"

"Right."

Jenny thought for a moment. "He said you're a well-known author."

"Embellishment."

"Do you write?"

"I try," David shrugged, "but I'm far from well known. Or even hardly known. I sell a few things, mostly commercial work. Greeting card lines. Advertising. Nothing of any real value."

"No novel?"

"Not done."

"No screenplay?"

"Don't know how."

"No book of poetry?"

"No soul."

The two exchanged expectant glances for a moment, then Jenny began to laugh, an infectious laughter David's intense relief allowed him to share.

"A beer, then?" He asked as the bartender arrived.

Armed with a glass of beer each, David and Jenny shared further accounts of Harry's eccentricities. As he began the account of a particularly ridiculous incident, David paused to listen to a change in the music being played.

"Hey, a slow song. Would you like to dance?"

"Certainly."

Jenny again displayed the smile that David had found so thoroughly captivating, and as they walked to the dance floor, David surreptitiously watched her. He studied her grace, amazed at how beautiful she looked and yet, uncontrollably, wondering how he could emulate that grace, how it would feel to be walking as she was, dressed as she was.

"I'm not really much of a dancer," he said as he slipped his arm around her waist, but he soon felt that he'd never been less clumsy than when he danced with Jenny Harris.

5.

The early morning Fourth of July sun had already confirmed predictions of a hot day when David parked his car in front of Jenny's apartment house. Before he could get out of the auto, his date bounded out of the doorway.

"I'm ready," she unnecessarily said as she slid in beside him.

"So I see," David answered, his eyes and attention fixed on the revealing nature of her swimsuit top.

"Isn't this appropriate?" she asked, glancing down at herself. "I am to wear a bathing suit, am I not? We are going to a beach, aren't we?"

"Beach. Right."

"Would you prefer I put this on?" From the gym bag she'd tossed on the seat, she produced a T-shirt bearing the logo of college she and Larry's wife had attended.

"No, not at all. You're fine. Wonderful." David put the car in reverse.

"Tell me," Jenny settled into the seat, "what is this mysterious place we're going to?"

"It's the ruins of the old McCormick family mansion up on the north shore. The McCormick Family." David explained. "The reaper, 'The Chicago Tribune.' Anyway, their old family seat is right on the lake just north of Fort Sheridan. Harry found it, or at least he's the one who introduced it to me. It used to be a huge estate and mansion, but now the buildings are all leveled and the grounds overgrown with woods. The stone outlines of reflecting pools are still visible, though, and there's a pavilion - I guess it had been a music pavilion - still standing. Through the woods, at the edge of the cliff overlooking the lake, there are the remains of a staircase that leads down to the water and the ruins of a swimming pool that was set right in the lake. Hardly anyone goes there. Actually, it's sort of against the law to trespass on the property. We have to park about a mile away and walk in through a residential neighborhood."

"Oh, great," Jenny feigned disgust, "the Fourth of July, and I'm going to get arrested. Why am I not surprised that Harry would discover something like this? I do have to go to work tomorrow, you know."

"We won't get arrested. As long as we walk in and don't park our middle class cars on the upper class streets, the police will ignore us."

Jenny spent a short time absorbing this information, then asked, "Who's Harry's date?"

"Goodness only knows. The wild woman of the week, I guess. She's bound to be interesting."

For about an hour they drove north on the tollway, speaking idly of the beauty of the day and of the things they'd done together over the preceding two months. David, occasionally and as unobtrusively as he could, studied Jenny's breasts in her bikini top. He found himself flipping between fantasizing about fondling them and about how it would feel if they were part of his own body.

After exiting the tollway, they passed through several highly affluent suburbs, eventually driving onto the campus of a small, clearly wealthy college and parking behind a hedgerow at the rear of one of the authoritative brick buildings. In the quiet summer hiatus few cars were present. Opening his car's trunk, David pointed out one of them.

"Harry's here already." As he extracted a large, full, olive drab army backpack, he added, "And here's our picnic basket. I've got some bratwursts, beer, and a blanket. The three 'B's."

"Very droll. In a backpack, though?" Jenny questioned.

"Certainly. A fourth 'B.' We have to walk a ways, and this makes it a bit less obvious that we are going to the beach."

"Right." Jenny gave him the smile for which he always waited and that stayed with him when they were apart. "It's much less suspicious that we appear to be heading for the jungle. Perfectly natural. And no doubt people in this neighborhood typically walk around the streets in bathing suits."

Jenny pulled the T-shirt from her bag, put it on, and the two putative non-beach goers set off walking along the sidewalk of a pristine neighborhood of relatively new, wildly ostentatious homes, each set on a large, neatly clipped and carefully watered lawn. Few cars passed, and they met no other pedestrians. After several minutes, rounding another of a series of artfully designed curves, they left inhabited homes behind, reaching a frontier of houses under construction, of scrub brush and trees. Ahead of them the road abruptly ended in weed covered Illinois prairie.

Just before they reached the end of the pavement, David suddenly veered off to the left, crossed the street, and led Jenny into a thick stand of trees. He walked quickly into the woods until the roadway was completely out of sight.

"We're safe now, right?" Jenny asked as she caught up to her date. "This is the forbidden forest?"

"We must be even more careful now," David looked about with exaggerated caution. "We're entering uncharted territory. Be very, very quiet and follow closely behind me."

"You're a strange man, David."

Jenny fell in behind him on a narrow, but well-worn path and followed him through the woods for perhaps fifty yards until he suddenly stopped and pointed into the trees.

"Ah ha," he whispered, "signs of the long-dead civilization of the lost Roman legion."

Jenny looked into the tangled undergrowth where David indicated and discovered, protruding several inches above the low ground cover, a curving line of sculpted concrete, the outline of a wide, gently curving oval that disappeared into the scrubby forest beyond.

"This is one of the reflecting pools," David explained. "There's another over that way." He pointed into the trees on the other side of the path. "I think the villa itself was just beyond that one. Down there," he indicated a path leading off to their right, "is the music pavilion. We can go see it later. The cliff and the beach are just ahead. Since Harry's there already, there's a good chance, if we approach quietly, that we can interrupt some weird activity."

A hundred yards farther on, the path emerged from the trees at the edge of a cliff beyond which the bright blue expanse of Lake Michigan stretched away to the eastern horizon. Jenny stood transfixed, unprepared, in spite of having seen it regularly for years from other perspectives, for the beauty and overwhelming magnitude of the lake before her, a panorama as impressive as an ocean shore. Viewed from a forested clifftop, the vast, empty lake seemed primeval. David put an arm around her shoulder and shared the inspiring sight to which he had led her.

Eventually, though, the sound of laughter floating up from the bottom of the cliff intruded on their quiet contemplation. They stepped to the edge and, looking down, saw the thin strip of sunlit beach on which several people were stretched out on blankets. Others were swimming in the gentle lake waves. David waved a greeting, then led Jenny to their left on a path gently descending the cliffside. They ducked under vines and over fallen trees, some dangling precariously over the receding cliff edge, clinging tenaciously to the top with half-exposed roots and seemingly determined to avoid or at least delay an obvious eventual fate. The pair reached the path's end at a crumbling semi-circle of paving stone. Set into the cliff wall to their left was a plaster and carved stone archway, long unused and blocked by the collapsed roof of a tunnel to which it had once given access. The archway's apex was decorated with a stone shield bearing in flourishing calligraphy the letter 'M.' To their right was the top of an ornate stone staircase.

The steps were bisected by a cement trough - down which a stream of water, spewing from the mouth of a carved dolphin, had once flowed - and were regularly interrupted by landings, each offering the respite opportunity of stone benches and requiring a turn toward the center to begin a new descent below a subsequent dolphin. The crumbling stone railings were decorated with carved whales and fantastic sea creatures, many of which elaborations remained intact, undisturbed by the passage of neglectful time and the creep of the reconquering forest. Jenny resisted David's hurry to reach the bottom. She descended slowly, marveling at the decaying opulence. She paused at each level to study the relief carvings and filigreed stonework.

Ten feet above the lake level they arrived on a wide, brick patio. Set into the cliff face beside the staircase was another stone archway blocked, as was its mate at the top of stairs, by the rubble of its collapsed interior. It too was crowned with an ornamental shield bearing the emblematic McCormick "M."

David approached the impenetrable tunnel and peered in. "It's the bottom of the elevator shaft," he explained. "Apparently the McCormicks could take an elevator from their gardens above down to the lakefront and the pool."

With nothing further to explore at the collapsed tunnel, David and Jenny walked across the brick patio, stepping out from the encroaching forest to stand at the edge of what had once been an enormous swimming pool set in and rising above the waters of the lake.

Cracked and crumbling, allowing lake waters to wash in and out, the pool nonetheless retained the outline of its perfect oval symmetry. The echoing gaiety of long dead party guests sunning themselves in lavish, servant-attended splendor seemed to linger around its edges.

Shouts of live party goers on the beach to their left, however, called Jenny and David back to the present, and they walked to the patio edge where another flight of stone stairs provided access to the sand below. Like the pool walls, the stairs had crumbled over time, making descent something of a scramble.

Harry splashed out of the water to greet them as they landed on the sand. "The beer's over there in the cooler," he pointed to a strip of shade at the base of the cliff, "and the grill's all fired up."

"Where's your date?" David asked.

"Christine." Harry almost seemed as though he were trying to recall his date's name. "Yes, Christine. She's out there in the water," he indicated a head bobbing in and out of sight in the waves. "She's trying to cool off. Obviously I'm far too exciting for her."

"Obviously."

Leaving Jenny with his friend, David dropped his backpack beside the cooler and deposited his beers into the ice, keeping two. After delivering Jenny's beer, he pulled from the backpack a crumpled, camouflage green mass that he shook out into blanket size and spread out on the sand.

"What in the world is that?" Jenny asked.

David gazed proudly at his offering. "It's the army's single greatest piece of technology: a poncho liner." He picked it up and handed it to Jenny. "See how light it is, and it can be folded up into practically nothing." Awaiting expression of amazement, he was disappointed, as Jenny simply turned it about a bit, then handed it back. "So, it's our beach blanket today." He spread it out again on the sand, and the two sat down to consume their first beers of the warm day.

By late afternoon, the sun had moved sufficiently west to cast the cliff's shadow across the entire beach, though the sand and the air remained comfortably warm. David and Jenny lay quietly on the poncho liner as other couples swam or wandered about the beach and the ruins.

"What a glorious day," Jenny said, turning on her side and draping an arm across her supine friend. "Thanks for bringing me here. It's a glorious place." Her fingers played with the hair on David's chest. "Have I told you how much I like hairy chests?" She tugged at a few hairs. "They're so masculine."

David pulled her head down and kissed her.

"I've never enjoyed myself more with anyone," he said, then hesitated. "I really love you, Jenny."

Without replying, Jenny rested her head on David's chest. Some moments later she suddenly stood up and looked across the seemingly limitless lake.

"Want to go back in the water?" David asked.

"No. I think I'd like to go see that music pavilion now. Can we?"

"Sure."

They pulled on their shoes, and David gathered up the poncho liner, compacting it as he had bragged into an easily carried mass. They walked along the beach to the crumbled steps and scrambled up the stones to the swimming pool deck where they found Harry and his date dangling their feet into the lake waves that replaced the former perfect, treated pool water.

"We're going exploring," David explained to the clearly unimpressed couple, obviously deeply engrossed in themselves.

"With your blanket," Harry observed.

"Yes," David deflected his friend's implication, "we're going to visit the pavilion and sit on its dusty stage."

He took Jenny's hand and led her away from the pool to the stairs. At the top, they retraced their earlier path along the cliff edge and into the woods, turning onto the pathway that David had indicated led to the pavilion. After a short walk through thick scrub, they came to a large clearing on the far side of which stood a strangely out of place but, even in decay, majestic structure consisting of a raised stage surmounted by a proscenium arch. Bas-relief carvings in various states of deterioration adorned the plaster façade, which bore at its very top the familiar shield and "M."

Crossing the weedy clearing, they walked around to the rear of the pavilion and, skirting a steep ravine that had encroached to within a few feet of the structure, climbed some steps to a doorless hallway lined with several rooms. Beyond these lay the stage, and they walked across the still solid wood floor to the front where David spread out the poncho liner so they could sit on the edge, beneath the overreaching arch. As they had earlier imagined the McCormick family's poolside party guests, they were able to conjure visions of elegantly clad audiences of the rich and privileged seated about a perfectly clipped lawn to be entertained by string quartets.

Leaning her head against David's shoulder, Jenny spoke softly. "About what you said on the beach, David..."

"Please," he cut her short, "don't say anything. I was too pushy. Forget I said it."

"O. K." Jenny's acquiescence was disconcertingly eager, and she let the subject drop, reaching her arms about his neck to draw him closer.

They kissed, lightly at first, then with more depth. Jenny pressed her body against his, and without having planned it, almost without thinking, David reached behind her back and, with a pull on the string, untied Jenny's bikini top. She reached up to hold it against her breasts, then leaned back and let it drop. In her face, as she looked at David, were confidence and pride that spoke of the significance of her act.

David uncontrollably experienced a thought of what it would feel like to have such breasts and to expose them as Jenny had just done, but he pushed it aside and drew her close. He pulled off his own shirt and eased Jenny onto her back.

6.

It was late and deeply dark when David and Jenny arrived in front of her apartment building. David turned off the car, and the two sat in awkward silence eventually broken by Jenny's allusion to the mundane.

"Work in the morning, David," she said. "I'm really tired, so I'm just going to head in. It's been a wonderful day."

She grabbed her bag and leaned over to kiss her date, but David made no reciprocal move.

"I understand," he rather mumbled. "I'm pretty beat, too. Sun, sand, and water are draining."

Apparently rebuffed, Jenny turned her back to the car door. "Is anything wrong?" she asked.

"No, of course not. Nothing at all." David seemed, however, uncertain, troubled. "Actually, everything is right. Really right. I was wondering... well, we've been together for months now. Since May. Months, but," he stumbled, "it seems like days. I want to ask you to... I wonder if you would consider..."

Jenny moved across the seat and kissed his cheek, stopping him. "David," she spoke forcefully, interrupting his halting progress, "it's been a big day. Let's talk tomorrow."

"It's not the beer," David turned with a sudden, earnest intensity. "It's not the beer or what we did…"

Again Jenny interrupted, this time placing a finger on his lips. "David, you point out that we've been dating since May. That's not really very long. It's early still, except that tonight, or rather, this morning, it's late, and I want to go in. We can talk some other time. Call me after I get off work, O. K?"

David nodded.

Jenny opened the car door. "Happy Fourth of July. Now a day late."

She stepped from the car and ran into the building. When she had disappeared, David, both tired and considerably deflated, shoved his gearshift into reverse and drove home.

He parked in his accustomed, somewhat isolated spot across the lot from his building and opened the car door to get out, but the arrival of another vehicle triggered his desire to remaining unseen by his neighbors, and he pulled the door shut.

A girl he had occasionally encountered in the lobby and hallway, apparently also getting home from an extended holiday night, stepped from her car and walked toward the building. David listened to the sound of her high heels on the pavement and admired her clothing.

"What a great dress," he thought, imagining that he was wearing it, walking in it.

Suddenly realizing the irreconcilable incongruity between these thoughts and those that had animated him so short a time earlier, he wrapped his arms around the steering wheel and cradled his head on them.

"I must be mad," he said aloud.

He remained in his car until the girl had entered the building, then ran across the parking lot, up to his apartment, along the hallway to his bedroom, and stood before the door to his closet.

Slowly, with an almost ponderous deliberateness, he exposed and unlocked the cabinet, confronting the clothing secured within. From the cabinet floor he picked up one high-heeled shoe of a pair and carried it to his bed where he sat contemplating the feminine footwear.

Suddenly, he grabbed his phone and began to dial Randy's number, but timely realization of the foolishness of the call, one he had rarely made other than at scheduled moments and one that at such an hour, could very likely be answered by Randy's wife, stopped him in time. He hung up and, holding the shoe, flopped back on his bed.

CHAPTER TWO

Three Sets

First Set

The Friday morning sun had yet to appear above the manufactured suburban horizon as David pounded through the last few hundred yards of his run. By getting out on the road with the first glimmering of morning light, BMNT - he still took some pride in identifying the moment by the infantry term, Beginning Morning Nautical Twilight - he could finish before the early August sun inflicted its punishing heat. He made the final turn south toward his home and slowed to a walk. Cooling down, he stopped and stretched before walking the two blocks back to his apartment.

As he bent from the waist to grasp his thighs, a house painting crew, similarly intent on a start that would beat the worst of the sun's heat, drove past, and one of the laborers called out, "Great legs, guy. They should be on a broad."

David waved at the truck's rear and, with a sincerity lost on the chuckling painters, shouted, "Thanks." Studying his legs, though, he reflected that the decision to resume shaving in the summer might require wearing sweat pants on his morning run.

Thoroughly stretched, he walked home and started the water in the shower, adjusting the temperature as he pulled off his running gear. He had just begun washing when the faint sound of the telephone penetrated that of the rushing water. Pulling back the shower curtain, he clearly heard the ringing phone and disgustedly stepped from the tub, grabbed a towel, wrapping it around himself and tucking it tightly beneath his armpits, and dripped along the hallway to his bedroom.

"Who would be calling so early?" he wondered as he reached for the receiver.

"David," the agitated voice on the line began, "it's Harry. You've got to help me. You've got to play tennis with me this morning."

Amazement supplanted curiosity. "Harry? What are you doing up this early? Or haven't you been to bed?"

"Yes, I've been to bed." Harry's tone betrayed impatience and frustration. "I'm up, and you've got to help me. Remember Walter Whalen, the Super Saver Marts owner?"

"Who won't sell your cookies," David recalled.

"Exactly. Well, remember also that you suggested I offer to play tennis rather than golf with him?"

"I do. That was months ago."

"Exactly again. I never give up. This week he accepted my offer to play at Oak Hills Country Club. He's bringing some employee this morning at eight and expects to play doubles against me and my plant manager, and my jerk partner just called to beg off. Some lame excuse about falling in the bathtub and breaking his wrist."

Sensing the direction the conversation was headed and that it might not be a short one, David sat on his bed and began to dry himself.

"David," Harry grew increasingly exasperated, "I've been trying to get our product in this man's stores for more than a year, and this match is the first time he's even been willing to spend any time with me. You've got to..."

"Harry, I'm going up to Wisconsin today. You know that."

"You can still go. We play at eight. You can be on the road by noon.

This could be a big account, David. Big."

"Big?"

"Very big. You've got to play. You're my buddy, my pal."

"All right, Harry, but I've got to be gone before noon. No beers after."

"Farthest thing from my mind. This is great. I'll pick you up at seven-thirty. See you."

"See you," David said to the buzz of an empty line, "and you're welcome."

He hung up the phone and completed drying himself, then grabbed a pair of sweat pants from the floor of his closet and, pulling them on, went quickly to the kitchen where he poured a bowl of cereal. At seven o'clock, breakfast eaten, he returned to the phone and dialed a number, smiling when a familiar male voice answered.

"Randy," Lynn spoke in a voice considerably softer than that with which David had earlier spoken to Harry, "it's Lynn. The family's gone?"

"Yes," Randy answered, "they left for grandma's bright and early this morning. Are you ready?"

"We have to alter our schedule, Randy." Lynn absentmindedly passed her fingers across the nipple of her left breast as she listened to the response her news elicited.

"We have reservations, Lynn," Randy said coolly. "We've planned this weekend for some time. Opportunities such as this are rare. I'm taking off work."

"I know. Don't worry. A friend of David's called this morning. He needs some help, and I couldn't refuse, but I'll be done by noon. You can pick me up at twelve-thirty. They'll hold the reservation 'till the evening, and we can be up there by four or five. It'll be fine."

"I guess it will have to be. Twelve-thirty, then."

"Thanks, Randy. I'll make it up to you."

David dug some socks, a T-shirt, and a pair of shorts from the jumble of clothes protruding from his closet floor. From beneath the bed he retrieved a pair of tennis shoes and a tennis racket. Fastening his hair into a ponytail, he dressed and headed back to the living room to wait for Harry. The image in the hallway full-length mirror, though, stopped him. He recalled the observation of the painters, and a thoughtful study of his hairless legs sent him back to the bedroom for the discarded sweatpants. His betraying legs covered, he settled onto the couch to await his friend's arrival.

At precisely seven-thirty the door buzzer sounded, and David went down to the lobby where Harry was nervously pacing.

"Hurry," Harry said as his friend stepped through the inner lobby door, "we've got to be at the Oak Hills courts before eight. Mr. Whalen believes in punctuality."

"They're only ten minutes away, Harry. And, Harry, relax. Everything will be just fine."

Harry pushed open the outer door, but stopped on the threshold and fixed his friend with a severe glare. "We can't be late, David," he said solemnly, "and we can't win, either. Do you see what I mean?"

"Yep."

"Nor," Harry started for the parking lot, "can it look like we're playing to lose. It has to look good."

"Harry, I understand, but this is really corny. It's a cliché, like something in an old movie."

"Cliché or not," Harry opened his car door, "it's deadly serious. There's a lot of money involved. If you'd ever get a real career you'd grasp this sort of thing."

"Yes, I suppose I would. But, I'm going to take my own car. That way I can just leave when we're done. You can be free to schmooze Mr. Whalen to your heart's content."

"Whatever. Just hustle."

Ten minutes later Harry led David past the guard shack at the country club, vouching for his friend in the trailing car and receiving the disturbing news that his other two guests had already passed through. They parked beside the tennis courts where Mr. Whalen and his partner were already warming up. As they swung open the fence gate, they saw the super market tycoon check his watch. Harry winced, then greeted his prospective business opportunity and introduced David, explaining the absence of his plant manager.

"You'd better not be bringing in a ringer, Harry," Mr. Whalen warned.

"A ringer? Oh, certainly not," Harry chuckled. David's just a fair player. Poor, actually."

"Horrible," David added with a wry smile.

The two friends moved off to the fence to set aside their bags and racket covers, and Harry watched with some interest as his doubles partner got ready to play.

"Aren't you going to take those off?" he asked, indicating the sweatpants David still wore.

"No."

"You're going to play in them?"

"Yes."

"Don't you have any shorts?"

"I have shorts, Harry." David grew a bit testy. "Do you think you'll lose the contract because Mr. Whalen can't see my legs?"

"Very humorous." Resigned, Harry followed David toward the net. "You'd think you'd cut your hair, though," he mumbled as they approached their waiting opponents.

After the new arrivals had enjoyed a few warm-up hits, Mr. Whalen and his partner won the racket spin and opened service. Fairly evenly matched, the two teams engaged in long, hard fought rallies through the first set, which the bearers of the Super Saver banner won 6-3.

"Great," Harry whispered to David as they passed around the net to begin the second set. "You're playing perfectly. It looks like they're really beating us."

"They are," David answered. "I haven't taken anything off my game, but we're going to win this set."

"What?" Harry's voice rose several octaves in panic. "Win a set? We can't do that. I thought you wanted to get on the road, Mr. Weekend in Wisconsin. Eight or nine games and you can go, and, if all goes well, I'll have a new contract."

"We can't just roll over, Harry. These two are experienced enough to figure it out. And I don't need to go so soon that I have to absorb a straight set loss. Besides, don't you see that Mr. Whalen is enough of a competitor that he'd prefer a close match?"

"A win, though. He has to have a win. Don't cut this too close."

David nodded and walked to the service line.

The second set was also closely contested, involving several deuce games, and Team Cookie Company won 6-4.

"You seem to have stepped it up, David," Mr. Whalen suggested across the net following set point. "You have a vicious down the line forehand."

"Thanks, Mr. Whalen."

"Call me Walt."

"Walt. Thanks."

"Well, it's match time, now."

With this pronouncement Mr. Whalen turned to confer with his teammate, and Harry pulled David to the rear of the court. "What did he say?" Harry pressed. "Did he sound happy?"

"Yes," David patted Harry's shoulder, "everything's fine. He's fired up about the third set."

"Which they'll win."

"Which they'll win," David said reassuringly. "I know the drill."

Harry's anxiety, however, increased as the game score advanced. During the changeover with his team up 4-2, he pleaded with his partner. "David, you've got to cooperate here. I'm losing my share of points. You've got to contribute."

"It's time." David wiped sweat from his brow and handed Harry two tennis balls. "Serve. I'm going to start taking the net more aggressively. Trust me," he offered in response to Harry's desperate look.

Harry dropped a rather weak serve across the court, and Mr. Whalen's partner returned the ball hard and low over the center of the net. Lunging wildly, David got a racket on the ball and sent it sharply into the tape.

"Fudge," he grumbled, batting the ball back into the net.

"'Fudge?'" Harry was stunned. "That's your excuse for profanity, 'Fudge?'"

"Just play, Harry."

David walked to the right service court as the players on the other side of the net chuckled over his child-like expletive substitute.

Throughout the next game and those following, David played with a reckless aggression that could have dominated, but several volleys he stroked from the net either sailed just wide or caught the tape. His tactic appeared perfect, but execution just off, off by such a small margin that it could not seem to have been fashioned by design, and the set and match went to the two grocers.

During the congratulatory handshakes, Mr. Whalen pointed out the obvious. "You got too anxious, David, too aggressive, and your volley deserted you. Also," Mr. Whalen grinned at his partner, "you've got to tone down that cursing."

"A great match, though," Harry interposed. "What do you say we go into the club for lunch and a few drinks courtesy of the losing team?"

"Thanks, Harry," David said, "but I've got to go. I'm already a bit behind schedule getting up to Wisconsin."

"You're going to Wisconsin today?" Mr. Whalen asked. "That's coincidental. So am I. But," he added, turning to Harry, "not without taking you up on that offer of lunch."

"Taking the family north for the weekend, then?" Harry inquired as the four left the court to gather their gear.

"Not exactly." Mr. Whalen offered Harry a tepid smile possibly suggesting some annoyance, then turned his attention back to David. "Good match, David. I enjoyed it. Thanks for filling in and saving Harry's rear end. You'll note that I can avoid profanity as well as you." Mr. Whalen gave a hearty laugh in which he was joined by his partner and Harry.

"My pleasure," David answered, shaking hands with the opposition. He gathered his racket cover and towel and headed for the gate where

Harry, having momentarily excused himself from his guests, caught up with him.

"Thanks, David," he whispered as he grasped his friend's arm. "Hey!" he looked at the arm he was holding and which David immediately pulled away. "Have you shaved your arms?"

"They're just that way, Harry." David turned away. "I've got to go."

Harry pondered a moment, then let it go. "I appreciate this," he refocused on the business he hoped to conduct. "You were great. Did you hear Mr. Whalen? You saved my rear end, he said. That sounds encouraging. And you can still get to Wisconsin on schedule. Are you taking Jenny?"

"No, I'm not taking Jenny."

"You're not? Now that I think about it, I haven't seen her much lately. Are you breaking up? It's not fall yet. The leaves haven't even begun turning."

David responded with requisite annoyance. "The season has nothing to do with it; we just decided to step back a bit. We still go out. You'd better go, or the 'big' contract is going to leave before you can steer him to lunch."

Harry looked anxiously back at Mr. Whalen and his associate who had collected their equipment and were obviously waiting for their host.

"You're right. I'll talk to you Monday. Thanks again." Harry tossed a hurried wave over his shoulder as he ran to rejoin the supermarket mogul.

David watched his exuberant friend congratulate the victors and begin to lead them in the direction of the clubhouse. Smiling to himself, he walked to his car.

Second Set

Back home, ascertaining the time with a quick glance at his bedroom clock, David tossed his tennis racket onto the bed and pulled off his clothes. He showered and, checking the smoothness of his legs and chest, shaved those places where hair could be felt. He carefully shaved his face, satisfied only when it felt completely hairless, and Lynn returned to her bedroom where she reached inside the doorjamb of her closet for the key to open the hidden wall locker.

From its floor she took a makeup case and, from a neatly arranged stack of lingerie, a brassiere and a pair of panties. She ran with this collection to the bathroom and, working hurriedly with the cosmetics, accomplished a conservative, but thoroughly convincing feminine appearance. She pulled on the panties and hooked the bra behind her back, filling its cups with two silicone breast forms taken from the makeup case.

With thorough enjoyment, then, she shook loose her shoulder length hair, which some careful pulls of a brush coaxed into a bouncy, feminine style. She paused a few moments to admire her handiwork before racing back to the bedroom.

Reaching once more into the cabinet, she pulled from a hanger a short, floral print summer dress and, from the floor, a pair of sandals. Fully dressed, she stood before the hallway's full-length mirror to appreciate her metamorphosis. Awareness of the time, however, once more cut short her study. From beneath her bed she extracted a previously packed suitcase, grabbed her tennis racket and carried them down the hallway, placing them beside the apartment door. After adding the makeup case from the bathroom to the luggage awaiting departure, she plopped onto the living room couch and swiftly applied polish to her fingernails.

The nail color had barely dried when the door buzzer sounded. Lynn ran to the intercom.

"Randy? Come on up." She pushed the lobby door button. "I'm all ready."

Lynn opened the apartment door and stood in the hallway, more to be seen by than to see Randy when he appeared at the top of the stairs.

"You look great, Lynn," Randy said with beaming pleasure as he walked along the hallway. When he reached her, the two embraced, and Lynn led her date into the apartment.

"Here," she said, indicating the items she had placed by the door. "You can take my suitcase and racket. I'll bring the makeup case, but first there's something I need to get from the bedroom. She went back down the hallway and returned holding high a plastic dress bag on a hanger. "My dress for tomorrow evening," she explained. "You'll be impressed."

Carrying the makeup case and long dress, Lynn followed Randy into the hallway, but as she was about to lock the door, she hesitated, looked at the racket Randy carried, and reopened the door. She grabbed the racket from his hand and gave him the dress bag.

"Oops. Just a minute. Minor error," she said. "I'll be right back."

Lynn ran once more down the hallway, tossed the tennis racket onto the bed and pulled another from the back of the wall locker. Returning to the hallway, she gleefully waved the new racket at the waiting Randy.

"Wrong racket," she smiled. "I almost brought a Stan Smith model. This," she wielded the new racket, "is my Chris Evert. We need to be gender consistent."

She started along the hallway, but Randy, rather than accompanying her, plopped his load on the floor, carefully draping the dress bag over the suitcase. He grabbed the wrist of the hand in which Lynn carried the racket and pulled her back, then gently gathered her other wrist and drew her close, pinning her hands behind her back.

"Hey," Lynn protested, "we've got to get going."

"You said this morning that they'd hold our reservations. You took the time to play tennis."

"You can't wait?"

"It's a long ride."

Lynn studied Randy's grin and then smiled back. "O. K.," she said, "you're in charge."

Randy released Lynn's arms, stooped to gather her luggage, and the two lovers went back inside the apartment.

Several hours later, sitting beside Randy as he drove his own British Racing Car Green Austin-Healy - rather than a rental car required as cover after a business trip flight - Lynn eagerly scanned the edge of a tree-lined and, other than for themselves, deserted road winding ahead of them through dense Wisconsin forest comprised of stands of trees oddly growing, courtesy of the depression era's Civilian Conservation Corps, in straight rows. Suddenly she broke what had been a protracted silence.

"There it is," she called out, pointing ahead to a white sign protruding from the trees on the right side of the road.

Randy slowed the car and turned into the narrow gravel driveway indicated by a sign bearing the single word "Xanadu." Closely flanked by pine trees, the drive wound up a gentle rise for about a half-mile, then abruptly emerged from the forest cover, bringing the two travelers onto a large, open hilltop.

Ahead of them, at the very top of the hill, stood a small hotel fashioned in the manner of a north woods lodge. Randy parked the car before a broad porch sheltered beneath a roof suspended on massive tree trunks. Across the porch a wide double doorway invited them in. He got out and walked around the car to open Lynn's door.

"Great legs," he offered as his weekend date stepped from the vehicle.

"So I've heard," Lynn, appreciating his appraisal, suggested as she wrapped an arm around one of his, snuggling next to him as they walked up the steps to the porch. From off to their right, the splashing and laughter of guests at play drew their attention to a swimming pool visible beyond a finely kept garden.

"I certainly hope they've held our reservations," Randy worried, indicating the lowering position of the sun in the western sky as they reached the heavy oak doors. He pulled one open and held it for Lynn. "It's a bit late to be driving back to Chicago."

They crossed large, oak floored lobby through which several couples, all male, were idly strolling. Two other guests, like Randy and Lynn apparently a male and female, were sitting together on a sofa before a huge, though in the warm summer inactive, fireplace. Lynn offered the pair an empathetic smile as she and Randy approached the reception desk, where she turned her attention to the cheery clerk as he greeted the newly arrived couple.

"And the name?" the clerk asked in response to Randy's inquiry concerning their reservation.

"Scott," Randy answered, "a room for two for tonight and Saturday."

The reservation had indeed been held, and, supplied with their room key and a schedule of the hotel's weekend events, Randy and Lynn headed back to the car for their luggage.

"Scott?" Lynn asked with some amusement as they stepped back into the slanting early evening sunlight.

"That's right."

Lynn considered the choice of name, soon making the connection.

"Scott. Of course. Randolph Scott."

"One of the great cowboys of all time," Randy proudly testified as he opened the trunk.

They carried the bags to the porch where Randy suggested Lynn wait while he moved the car to the guest parking lot. As he and the car disappeared around the corner of the lodge, Lynn waved, then walked quietly about the porch, looking over the pleasantly lush grounds of the resort. Two men in swimming trunks and with towels draped over their shoulders pushed out of the lobby door, were apparently surprised by encountering Lynn, and, scowling, veered a bit as they crossed the porch enroute to the swimming pool. Her back to the doorway, Lynn failed to notice this questionable encounter and remained happily content, enjoying the breeze that ruffled her skirt against her bare legs.

When Randy returned, bounding around the corner of the lodge, he came up behind Lynn and put his arms around her, enhancing her quiet happiness.

"Let's go on in," he suggested.

They picked up the luggage and soon found their room.

"The dinning room is open," Lynn, referring to the schedule provided by the desk clerk, announced as they began to unpack. "When do you want to go down?"

"How late do they serve?"

"Till nine."

"Good." Randy pulled some sweat clothes from his suitcase. "I think I'd like to go down to the weight room and work out a bit first. I'm stiff from the long drive. Want to come?" Carrying his athletic clothes, he disappeared into the bathroom.

"No," Lynn answered. "I'm pretty tired. I've been up since 0-dark thirty and I did play three sets of losing tennis this morning. I think I'll get a nap in while you're gone."

Suited up for his workout, Randy returned to the bedroom and discovered Lynn wearing a nightgown and settled on the bed for a nap.

"You don't mind if I go?" he asked.

"Randy, I'm trying to nap."

"Don't disappear while I'm gone."

"Ah," Lynn grasped his meaning. "You'd better see to it that I don't, then."

She held out her wrists, and Randy dug through a pouch in his suitcase, extracted a length of cord with which he tied Lynn's wrists together, tying its end to the headboard of the bed, leaving her enough rope to move about somewhat freely. He kissed her, then, grabbed the room key, waved and slipped out the door.

Sometime later, extremely sweaty, Randy again sat on the bed beside Lynn. He gently awakened her.

"Good workout?" she asked.

"Not bad. It's a kind of small facility, but not bad. I talked to a guy who'd like to play some tennis. He's here with a regular partner, I gather, and they're looking for a doubles match."

"So, we're playing?" Lynn pushed her bound hands under Randy's shirt.

"Yes, if you want. First thing in the morning. We have the court for seven o'clock.

A bit more awake, Lynn showed more interest in Randy's news.

"Did you tell him we're a mixed doubles team?"

"Yes. He was a bit hesitant, but I assured him you can play, and he seemed content."

Though somewhat unconvinced by Randy's reassurance, Lynn shrugged, yawned, and stretched out luxuriantly.

"Tired?" she asked.

"A bit."

"Ah, too bad."

The two exchanged knowing glances as Lynn curled her body around her lover.

"But not that tired." Randy untied the cord fastening Lynn's wrist to the headboard, pulled it shorter, drawing her arms above her head, and retied it. From his suitcase he secured several more lengths of the cord and pulled her ankles to the foot of the bed, tying each to a corner.

Early the next morning, fresh from a shower and thoroughly shaven, Lynn stepped into a short tennis dress and gathered her hair into a ponytail that she held on top of her head while Randy pulled up the dress' zipper. Ready for the morning's match, the two lovers eagerly ran down the stairs to the lobby, Lynn enjoying the sight of her long legs exposed beneath the abbreviated tennis dress. As they walked through the colorful and aromatic flower garden, they saw two men warming up, already in possession of the center court.

Lynn stopped suddenly and turned her back to the courts, seizing Randy's arm to halt him. "Are those the guys?" she asked.

Randy looked over her shoulder at the men. "Well, the big guy is Walt, the one I met last night. The other must be his partner, so I guess they are. Is there a problem?"

"Your buddy Walt," Lynn grabbed Randy's shirt and pulled him close, "is Walter Whalen, wealthy owner of six Super Saver Marts and the man with whom David and his friend Harry played tennis yesterday morning."

Randy again gazed beyond Lynn's shoulder at the two men pounding a ball back and forth across the net.

"So what? We're here, and he's obviously here for much the same reason. He's not going to alert the media about you. Come on, let's play."

Lynn grabbed Randy again, stopping his attempt to continue to the court.

"It's not that simple," she urged. "I don't want him to recognize me. It could hurt my friend's business."

"I don't imagine he could recognize you. You do, after all, look a bit different, and it's not exactly the sort of thing one would expect. Besides," Randy smiled into the distance beyond Lynn and waved, "they've seen us. We've got to go."

Still Lynn held him. "This is crazy," she said. "He's here with a man."

"As are you."

"But, he's married."

"As am I."

"Yes, but I'm sure his problem isn't that his wife won't let him tie her up."

Randy scowled at his partner.

"All right, then, fine," Lynn capitulated, "but wait just a minute." She handed her racket to Randy and pulled the tie from her ponytail, shaking her hair about her head. "I wore a ponytail yesterday, so maybe this will help." She sighed. "Let's do it."

They walked on to the court where Randy and Walt handled the introductions. Walt and his partner were clearly uneasy about meeting Lynn, uncertain about shaking her hand. Angered, Lynn, as she and Randy placed their gear against the fence, threw her racket cover down.

"So," she whispered, "they don't like playing with a girl like me, I guess. Let's destroy them."

As the two teams exchanged warm-up hits and practice serves, Lynn demonstrated a level of ability that seemed to mollify her opponents, and soon the joy of the sport blurred any question of gender or appearance, leaving only the spirit of athletic competition. Just as Randy played a better game than Harry, Walt's Wisconsin partner proved to be superior to his business associate, and the match gradually generated a greater intensity than had the previous day's. The teams traded wins in the first two sets, and during a changeover in the third, Lynn pulled Randy close to whisper to him.

"All right," she said, "up 3-2. Hold service here, Randy, and we've got them." She held his arm affectionately, but with a firmness of purpose.

"It's just a game, Lynn," Randy reminded her. "We're supposed to be having fun."

"I threw a match to this guy yesterday, Randy, and I want this one as payback. Besides, they were so offended to be playing against me. No mercy. No quarter."

Lynn set up in the forecourt, and Randy smashed a strong first serve deep into the service court corner. Walt's partner lunged and sent a weak return barely over the center of the net.

Lynn stepped into the shot and got her racket on the ball for an easy kill, but drove it hard into the tape, and the ball dropped at her feet.

"Oh, fudge!" she groaned as she sagged in disappointment. She stooped to pick up the errant ball and when she rose, found herself confronting the rather large figure of Walt Whalen looming just across the net. He was staring at her.

"Fudge?" he repeated.

"Well," Lynn avoided his gaze, "I really meant something else, but it wouldn't have been ladylike." She tossed the ball back to Randy and walked along the net to the other service court. Without looking, she could feel Walt, who remained motionless at the net, watching her.

Randy held service for a 4-2 lead, and then he and Lynn won the next two games to take the set and match.

"Good match," Walt congratulated his opponents as the four players shook hands across the net. "That was a pleasant surprise."

"Surprise?" Lynn shot back.

"Yes." Walt made a gesture that included his partner. "We didn't really expect to find such stiff competition here. I greatly enjoyed the match. I played one yesterday that I suspect my opponents purposely dropped. This was far more enjoyable."

Randy put an arm around Lynn's shoulders and quickly redirected the conversation. "It was fun," he admitted, "and now I'm hungry. Who's for getting some breakfast?"

"Not me, thanks," Lynn patted her stomach. "A girl's got to watch her waistline, you know. You go on ahead," she suggested to Randy. "I'm going to get a shower." She looked across the net at the two defeated opponents. "I, too, enjoyed the match. Thanks for your consideration in letting me play," she added with apparently undetected sarcasm.

Walt, his partner, and Randy watched Lynn while she gathered her gear and pushed through the court gate, then collected their own equipment and walked together to the hotel to have a morning meal.

Randy and Lynn avoided reference to the match until that evening when, rummaging through a small overnight bag he had brought, the former addressed his partner's behavior.

"You didn't have to be so hostile, you know," he suggested, pulling out of the bag the copy of "The Chicago Tribune" for which he had been searching.

"You have today's paper?" Lynn, sitting beside him on the edge of the bed, drawing a stocking over her right foot, was a bit amazed.

"It's yesterday's, but I haven't read it yet. I don't want to miss the local news just because I'm in Wisconsin."

"Astounding. But what are you talking about, 'hostile?'"

"When you left the court. They meant no disrespect."

Lynn thrust her leg out straight and drew the stocking up to her thigh. "Oh, please, Randy. I'm sick of gays demanding to be included in mainstream society, throwing tantrums, insisting on 'equal rights,' whining about being victims of prejudice, then inflicting on people like me the same intolerance they decry. They'll be advocating for gay marriage rights, but will be horrified if one of us wears a bridal gown. It's so hypocritical."

"I don't think our tennis opponents are particularly gay rights advocates and I don't think they were offended by you; just unfamiliar."

"Perhaps you're right." Lynn pulled a stocking onto her other leg, fastening its top with the hook of a garter belt, and stood beside the bed, looking down at the recumbent Randy.

"Did Walt say anything that would suggest he recognized me?"

"No, but if he did spot you, your petulance certainly didn't help David's friend."

"Aren't you going to get ready?" Lynn ignored the criticism. "The dance starts in a half-hour."

"I'll be ready. I just want to read the paper. It won't take long."

"I don't believe this. Do you read it everyday?" Lynn walked to the closet from which she retrieved her dress bag.

"Without fail."

"Well, I'm going to dress. I can't wait for you to see this gown. And me in it."

She went into the bathroom and about fifteen minutes later called out, "Ready?"

Randy indulgently lowered his paper. "Yes, indeed," he answered, "I'm ready. Let's have it."

Lynn excitedly framed herself in the bathroom doorway, posing exuberantly, twirling so Randy could see everything. She had pinned her hair up in a formal style that left curled ringlets dangling about her face and wore a black, floor-length gown, slit provocatively up one side to mid-thigh. Her arms were encased in black opera length gloves.

Randy was satisfactorily appreciative. "Beautiful," he said softly as he set the "Tribune" aside and rose to walk over to her. He took one of her hands and turned her slowly about to inspect more closely. "Beautiful," he repeated, and his pleasure was reflected in Lynn's beaming smile. He drew her close, and they kissed, but then Lynn pulled away.

"So come on," she importuned, "get dressed. I want to go down to the dance and ...dance." Randy went back to the bed.

"Just a couple more pages and I'll be done. Only the editorial section. Wait just a bit."

"Not a chance," Lynn replied. "I'm all set, ready to splash my brilliance across the world. Or at least the hotel. I've been waiting too long for a chance to dress up like this and I'm not going to squander the time. Remember, you're responsible for this. Just last summer I wouldn't have been me at all. Now I'm taking every moment I can get, so hurry up. You can meet me in the bar."

"I could tie you to the chair; then you'd have to wait. Those gloved wrists would look great bound."

Lynn took a small evening bag from the dresser and went to the door where she assumed a stance that opened the dress' slit, exposing her leg to the top of her stocking.

"There will be no wrinkling of this dress until I've been out in it. Hurry on." She waved and left the room.

Softly humming "I Feel Pretty" from *West Side Story*, Lynn strode smoothly, gracefully down the hallway to the elevator. Walking through the lobby, she listened to the sound of her high heels on the wooden floor and felt the flowing pull of her long dress against her legs. She was conscious that glances from men she passed, though probably devoid of sexual appreciation, seemed nonetheless complimentary, and she happily reflected that outside in the world beyond the grounds of "Xanadu" other men, for other reasons, would also watch her sensual passage and, unaware of the truth, lust for her.

At the entrance to the bar, she paused to adjust to its subdued light. Music from the jukebox was playing, and the dance floor was filled with couples, none of which appeared to be of mixed gender. Soon confident of her path, she weaved through the scattered tables to an empty stool at the end of the bar and discovered, after settling onto the seat, that the expansive back of the man sitting next to her, but unaware of her arrival, was that of Walt Whalen.

"Hello, Walt," she said as she placed her bag on the bar.

The man turned and, recognizing her, registered mild surprise.

"Hello, Lynn. It is Lynn, is it not? You look quite different."

"I'll take that as a compliment," Lynn smiled as the bartender arrived. She ordered a Vodka and Seven-Up, and glanced around the room. "Where's your friend?" she asked.

"He took a drive into town." Walt continued to examine Lynn's gown. "That's an attractive dress. It looks rather expensive," he suggested. "Where did you get it?"

"I didn't steal it from a clothesline, if that's what you suspect. I shop like anyone else. This came from a catalog. Walt," Lynn leaned toward him and lowered her voice, "I want you to understand. The point here for me is to be a woman. To be reminded that one isn't rather spoils the effect."

"Sorry," Walt tepidly offered as the bartender delivered Lynn's drink. "I just thought someone I know might like it." He watched her begin to fish through her purse for some money, then, impatient, pushed some bills across the bar.

"Here. I'll buy the drink as an apology. And because the bartender can't wait all night."

Lynn smiled and raised her glass in gratitude.

"I see Randy wears a wedding ring," Walt said, rather startling Lynn. "Is that part of your image? You don't wear one."

Lynn set her drink on the bar and looked disapprovingly at her interlocutor. "I'm sure you know better than to ask about people's lives outside of here, Walt."

"It seemed harmless." He took another direction. "Are you exclusively his…partner?"

"Why?" Lynn became playful. "Are you interested?" She placed a hand on one of his, which he withdrew. "Now I'm sorry," she lamented. "I didn't mean to be flippant. Randy and I have known each other for nearly a year. We met one evening at 'Charlie's.'"

"Who's Charlie?"

"Not who, what. You've never heard of it, then? It's famous, sort of. In certain circles, anyway, I guess. It's a bar kind of hidden away in one of the northwest suburbs of Chicago, a place for girls like me to hang out. We're welcome there. Anyway, Randy came there looking for - what he was looking for; we met and we've been sort of exclusive since."

"Sort of?"

"Well, in this context."

Walt finished his drink and turned to face Lynn more directly. His eyes strayed to her neckline, an interest she noted.

"You're doing it again," she admonished.

"Doing it again?"

"Failing to play the game. You're wondering how much is me. You're supposed to pretend it all is."

Walt twisted his stool back to the bar and indicated to the bartender his need for another whiskey. "I'm just not used to people like you, I guess. I certainly didn't mean to be rude or inappropriate."

The two sat in silence for a few minutes while Walt waited for his drink. When it had arrived and he had paid for it, Lynn directed his attention to the song playing on the jukebox. "Would you dance with me?" she asked.

Walt looked over his shoulder at the filling dance floor and shook his head. "No, I think not."

Lynn rose from her stool and more insistently tugged on Walt's arm. "I insist," she importuned. "You bought me a drink, now you must dance with me. It's a house rule."

Walt considered, clearly reluctant, but with a resigned grimace, rose and led the way to the dance floor at the edge of which he hesitated.

"It's just the same," Lynn instructed, putting her left hand on his shoulder and taking his left hand with her right. "See?"

They danced rather awkwardly at first, and Lynn moved herself closer to her unenthused partner, pressing her body against his and reaching farther behind his neck.

"It's easy," she said softly, "just lead me around as you would any woman."

"So you assume I've spent time with women?"

Lynn realized that, though an impression remained, Walt had

removed his wedding ring. However, appreciating the potential indiscretion, and declining to allude, as had Walt earlier, to wedding rings, Lynn attempted to deflect the conversation.

"Just an assumption. You mentioned a friend who might appreciate my dress. I could be wrong."

She mingled her feet with his, bringing their legs into contact, and, as they danced, she felt Walt gradually relaxing, taking charge and proving to be a quite accomplished dancer. He twirled her about, and she enjoyed the feel of her long dress as she stepped quickly to follow.

"That wasn't so bad, was it?" she asked when the song had ended. "You're an excellent and obviously experienced dancer."

"But as you say," Walt headed back to the bar, "that is a matter we should not discuss."

When they had regained their seats, Lynn spotted Randy at the doorway, obviously searching the crowd for her.

"Ah, here's Randy at last." She waved frantically to attract his attention.

"We've just been dancing," Lynn informed him when he had joined her and discovered Walt's presence. "It was great fun. Now, though," she announced to Walt, "Randy and I are going to the ballroom. Perhaps you and your friend, when he returns, would care to join us." She thanked him for having bought her drink, took Randy's arm and, clinging closely to him, left the barroom.

Third Set

Early the following Monday evening, while Lynn, wearing a tank top and a long, flouncy full skirt, lay on her couch reading a book, Harry called. He was even more urgent than he had been the previous Friday morning.

"David," he began as soon as Lynn had lifted the receiver, "you've got to help me."

A bit disappointed to have to give way to David, Lynn responded in his voice. "Again I have to help you, Harry. Couldn't you just say, 'Hello?"

"Hello. Now listen. It's Whalen again."

David tensed, concerned about what news his friend might have to relate.

"I thought we had blown it last week." Harry was excited. "After you left, Whalen just snarfed down a burger and made some lame excuse to bug out. He just hedged around about the cookies, wouldn't really discuss business. I figured we'd blown it."

"And we hadn't?"

"Whalen called me at the office this morning. He wants to play again and he made it particularly clear that he wants you to play."

David said nothing.

"David," Harry practically shouted into the phone, "are you listening? You've got to help me."

"When does he want to play?"

Harry's relief was perceptible. "Friday evening. Seven o'clock. At the Oak Hills courts again. You'll play?"

"I'll play."

"Great. Wonderful. Thanks, David. You're a prince. Want me to pick you up? We can go out hustling women after I wrap up the deal."

"No, I'll just see you there."

"Great. And, David, do you think you could..."

"No, Harry, I couldn't cut my hair. And I'll be wearing sweat pants. Hang up, now."

Lynn set the phone back down and slowly walked back to the living room sofa. She sat down and, ignoring the book she had set aside, considered the implications of Harry's news. She reasoned that she must have escaped detection in Wisconsin and assumed that consequently another meeting with Walter Whalen would be safe.

That Friday evening David drove his car to the gate of the country club and, upon invoking Harry's name, was waved on by the guard.

Approaching the courts, he saw the other three men - Harry, Mr. Whalen, and the latter's partner from the previous week — warming up.

"You're late." Harry met him just inside the fence. "No matter, but hurry up."

Mr. Whalen reached out his hand to David as the latter stepped up to the net. "It's good to see you again," he said. "I'm glad Harry could prevail upon you to join us. Perhaps today your volley won't desert you."

David nodded, apprehensively watching for any hint that Walt connected him with Lynn, the doubles opponent from Wisconsin, but if he did, he hid it well.

After allowing David a few hits to warm up, the four men began to play, and the match proceeded much as had the previous week's, the teams splitting the first two sets and holding service through the first eight games of the third.

"This is great," Harry, gathering balls for his service game, chuckled to his partner. "Whalen seems in a good mood. After we lose, we'll hit the club for a few drinks, and I'll clinch the deal." Harry fairly cackled with glee.

"We're going to win, Harry," David calmly announced.

"What?" Harry seized David's arm, glanced briefly at it, then let it go. "We can't win."

"Well, O. K., we may not," David wiped sweat from his face, "but if we don't, it won't be because we threw it."

"David," Harry was incredulous, "are you trying to destroy me? Is that it? You hate me. It's about that girl I set you up with last year, isn't it? I tell you I didn't know she was that disturbed."

"Harry," David placed a reassuring hand on his friend's shoulder, "Whalen will know if we take a dive. Trust me. He'll be happier losing, if he knows it was an honest match."

"Oh, and I suppose you've discussed it with him?"

David paused, looking intently at his friend. "I assure you I'm right," he finally stated. "Come on, let's get them."

Dejected, but with a sigh of resignation, Harry stepped to the baseline and began his service game. Surprisingly, to his partner, he served well and with a 40-15 lead sent a hard serve deep into the service court. Off balance, Mr. Whalen looped a soft return over the center of the net, allowing David to drive a volley past him into the corner for the game.

"So," Mr. Whalen congratulated David on the shot, "it seems you brought your net game today."

The next game, the set, and the match went to team Cookies, and the four men gathered at the net to shake hands.

"Good match," Mr. Whalen offered, "I enjoyed that. I had thought that we probably caught you on an off day last week, David."

"It was fun, wasn't it," Harry was a bit tentative. "What do you say we take a rest on the club veranda? I'll order some drinks."

"Sorry, Harry," David demurred, "I can't stay."

Mr. Whalen intervened. "Join us for at least one, David. You should be with us as," he clapped an arm around Harry's shoulders, "Harry and I arrange a Monday meeting to discuss placing his product in our stores. It's a bit, after all, of your own doing, anyway."

Having apparently settled the question, Mr. Whalen led the way to the clubhouse. Harry cast an incredulous grin back at David and motioned to his friend to follow along.

"Oh, fudge," David chuckled to himself as he gathered his gear and set off in hurried pursuit of the others.

CHAPTER THREE

A Night at the Movies

"In an hour?" Contemplating the muddle of papers strewn about her kitchen table and crumpled on the floor, the frustrating result of an incapacity to coherently advance the story on which she had been working, Lynn was hesitant, but quickly recovered, both welcoming the unexpected interlude with her lover and accustomed to the uncertainty that characterized his opportunities to spend time with her. "Of course. Come on over. I have a new little black dress you haven't seen. I'll be waiting."

Happy, upon reflection, for the opportunity to escape from her literary miasma, Lynn collected the rejected papers from the floor and tossed them into a wastebasket, then pushed the stacks of work to be saved into a semblance of organization and placed them in the wooden box that served as her filing cabinet.

She ran along the hall to her bedroom where she pulled off the grubby sweatshirt she was wearing and the brief athletic shorts, tossing them both into the corner of her closet beside the cabinet, which stood, as had become her practice, unhidden, unlocked, and open. She gathered and tossed onto her bed some stockings, a garter belt, shoes, and her makeup case, then, with some deference, removed a hanger on which was hung a short, simple black dress. Holding it at arm's length, she studied the dress with happy anticipation before collecting the other items and carrying them all to the bathroom.

A half-hour later, clad in the dress and high heels, and happily pleased with the results of her cosmetic handiwork, Lynn was contemplating applying some nail polish when the door buzzer sounded. She ran to the intercom and pressed the button.

"You're a bit early," she announced, "but I'm just about ready. Come on up."

"Ready for what?" an unexpected voice responded. "Early for what? Is that you, David? What apartment is this?"

"Harry?" Stunned, Lynn immediately altered her voice. "What are you..." she quickly formed a course of action. "Come on up." She pressed the door button. "I'm taking a shower. Just come on in. I'll leave the door open."

She pushed open the apartment door and raced back to the bathroom where she kicked off her shoes and turned on the shower. Reaching behind her back, she struggled to unzip her dress. As it fell to the floor, she heard the apartment door close and Harry walk to the kitchen and, presumably, the refrigerator. Opening the bathroom door a crack to offer Harry a beer, she heard the pop of an opened bottle.

"Just get a beer," David called unnecessarily, "I'll be right out."

"Ready for what?" Harry asked.

"What are you talking about?" Lynn was rapidly removing her feminine garments, dropping them on the floor about her feet.

"You said you were almost ready."

"Almost Ready? Oh, right. I'm always almost ready. You know me."

Lynn shut the door completely and filled the sink with hot water. Working at a frantic pace, she thoroughly scrubbed her face with cold cream, reflecting on how fortunate it was that she hadn't put on nail polish. A careful check in the mirror convinced the emerging David that all visual traces of Lynn had been erased. He sought to mask any lingering aroma of perfume with a liberal application of aftershave lotion.

He shut off the shower water and wrapped a towel around himself, tucking it tightly beneath his armpits, then, realizing his error as he reached for the doorknob, refastened the towel around his waist and stepped into the hallway.

"I'll be right there," he said as, being careful to turn his shaved body from Harry's view, he ran to the bedroom. Tossing aside the towel, he pulled on a pair of blue jeans and a sweatshirt. Male once again, David attempted to adopt a casual naturalness as he sauntered back along the hallway.

"Get yourself another beer, if you're ready" he suggested, but upon reaching the kitchen, he found Harry already extracting two bottles from the refrigerator.

"Whoa!" Harry shook his head as he handed, at arm's length, one of the beers to his friend. "Are you modeling after-shave?"

"A bit much?"

"You may be driving the entire population of DuPage County east to the lake."

"I thought you were going out with Christine tonight."

"I was, but she's sick," Harry explained as he strolled into the living room and settled onto the couch. "You know, David, I'm beginning to think I should get married. That way, even if Christine is sick, I'm not missing a date."

David followed his friend into the living room, but paced nervously across the face of the patio doorway. "That doesn't make any sense."

"Nonetheless, pal, I believe I am going to ask Christine to marry me." Harry took a long drink from his beer. "And I believe you should get married, too. We're certainly getting past the normal age, getting over-ripe. We may cease being marriage material. I kind of thought you and Jenny were headed that way. What's happening with that? You should marry her and give me a report."

"Actually, I nearly proposed once."

"Nearly? No kidding. Is she aware of that?"

"I think so. It was on the Fourth of July, when we went up to the McCormick mansion. I suspect she knew. Actually, I think she stifled it."

"That was a great day. Now that I think about it, that was my first date with Christine. But you've never told me about this proposal. What happened?"

David continued pacing. "Nothing. As I say, she sort of shut it down before I could really get going. It hasn't come up again. My guess is she doesn't conceive of me as serious. Not, as you say, marriage material."

"And so that's why the relationship has cooled. I thought it was just the arrival of September. Cooler autumn weather. Well, anyway," Harry ignored his friend's disgusted glare, "since I probably can't find anyone to propose to tonight, I thought maybe you'd like to go see 'Bananas.' It's playing second run at The Tivoli theater."

"I'd like to see it, but a guy I know from...work is stopping by, and we..."

"Work? What work? You don't work."

"Cut it out, Harry. I work. It's someone from the agency that occasionally gives me assignments."

Harry was nonplussed, "We could all go. I have no objections to agency men."

The discussion was cut short by the door buzzer announcing another visitor. David sprang to the intercom and in an almost cartoonishly deep, masculine voice, spoke loudly and rapidly, precluding any response from the person downstairs.

"Hello, this is David. David here. Is this Randy? It's David. Come on up and meet my friend, Harry, who is also here."

The antic behavior drew a quizzical look from Harry. "And you call me weird," he commented as his grinning host stepped into the hallway.

David watched the empty corridor and, when Randy appeared at the top of the stairs, signaled for silence and directed Lynn's puzzled date to precede him into the apartment.

"A bit much on the after-shave, isn't it David?" Randy said, emphasized the masculine name as, leaning away as much as he could, he squeezed past through the doorway.

"This is my friend Harry," David announced as he and Randy entered the living room. "We went to college together. You've heard me speak of him. I've explained that you work for the ad agency downtown and that we were going out for some beers.' Harry wants to go see 'Bananas' tonight."

Harry rose from the couch and shook Randy's hand. "So you try to help the struggling Herman Melville out with some assignments, I hear."

"Yes, I do. I have assignments." Randy cast an annoyed look at David.

"I'll get you a beer, Randy," David intervened. "Are you ready, Harry?"

Harry indicated his still half-full bottle, sending David off for just one. As he returned to the living room with Randy's drink, the door buzzer sounded a third time.

"Now who?" David handed Lynn's frustrated lover his beer and walked to the intercom, offering an abrupt, "Yes?"

"Well," Jenny's startled voice came out of the speaker, "Pardon me for wanting to see you."

"Jenny. Come on up. Join the party," David smiled weakly to the pair in the living room and pushed the door release. "It's Jenny."

Randy nodded.

"I've sort of been dating her for a while."

"Almost married her," Harry said.

"Indeed?" Randy replied.

"It's autumn, though," Harry continued as, impervious to David's threatening grimace, he made his way to the refrigerator, "so he's cooled off. I'll get one for Jenny."

"Oh." Jenny, entering the apartment, was surprised to see Randy, someone she did not know, in the living room. "I didn't know you had company. What's that smell?" She tentatively tested the air around David. "It's your after-shave, isn't it, David? It's very nice, but you've used a bit much."

Harry emerged from the kitchen, holding out a bottle of beer to Jenny.

"And you're here, too, Harry. Is this a party?" She took the beer from Harry and walked into the living room where David introduced her to Randy.

"I was just driving home," she explained to David, "and had the thought that if you weren't doing anything in particular, we could see Woody Allen's 'Bananas' at The Tivoli."

"That's just what I was thinking," said Harry, who had made another sortie to the refrigerator and was returning munching on piece of cold pizza.

"You're hungry," David observed. "Of course you are. Probably we all are. I have more pizza I could warm up and some chips and stuff. Sit, everyone. I'll get some food."

He went around the corner into the kitchen and pulled several half-full bags of potato chips from the cabinets. When he turned around from the refrigerator with a frozen pizza, he found Randy hovering beside him.

"So how are you going to handle this?" Randy asked in a whisper. "You know these nights are hard to come by. I didn't come here to eat pizza and watch a movie."

"I know, Randy," David answered softly. "Lynn was all dressed and ready when Harry arrived. I'll find a way to get out of the movie plan. They can go together, and when they've gone, we can get back on track."

"And I suppose you're embarrassed to know a management consultant."

David attempted to emphasize his sincerity without raising the volume of his whisper. "No, certainly not. I just had to think of some plausible way I would know you. I couldn't very well say we'd met at 'Charlie's,' could I?"

"By the way," Randy leaned a bit closer, but, repelled by David's after-shave, stepped back again, "how do you explain your completely shaven body to this Jenny woman?"

"What makes you think she sees my complete body?" David tried to be coy, but Randy's impatience was apparent. "O. K.," David conceded, "swimming."

"Swimming?"

"Yes. Since I started shaving again, I've taken up swimming. It's a perfect cover. I just point out that being hairless improves my lap speed. She knows I'm a bit competitive."

"And she buys this?"

Before David could answer, Jenny bounced into the kitchen.

"Hey," she cheerily announced, "we could all go to the movie. Harry's checking the time, but I think we have to get moving. I need to use your bathroom, David."

"Sure." David's attention was focused on Randy's reaction to this proposal, but as he saw, out of the corner of his eye beyond Lynn's unhappy lover, Jenny moving toward the bathroom, he remembered what lay scattered about that room's floor.

"Wait," he shouted, pushing his way around Randy. "Stop!" He grabbed Jenny's arm just as she reached the bathroom door. "Don't go in there."

"Why not? Can't I use it?"

"Of course you can use it. It's just that it's...dirty. Yeah, dirty. I left a whole ton of dirty underwear around."

"David," Jenny leaned close to whisper, but, like Randy before her, was repelled by David's after-shave. Still, she spoke softly. "I've seen your underwear."

"No, no," David insisted, "It wouldn't be right. Just let me straighten up."

He opened the door just enough to edge through and shut it behind him. Inside, he quickly gathered up Lynn's discarded clothing and stuffed it into his dirty clothes hamper, covering it with towels that had been left about. He replaced all the cosmetics into their case and shoved that behind the toilet paper and cleaning solutions in the cabinet beneath the sink, then, after a swift, but thorough final check, opened the door and stood aside.

"Much better. It would have been too embarrassing." He grinned as Jenny passed by.

"So," he resumed his clandestine conversation with Randy, "I'll get them to go to the movies on their own. We can still have a full evening. You'll see."

"No," Randy looked resigned. He dropped an empty beer bottle into the trash and moved toward the apartment door. "This is pretty well shot. I'm supposed to be driving home from Iowa tomorrow morning, but if I just go home now, I can score some points for getting home early. It'll be good cover for the future. We'll just have to set up another time when we can." Addressing Harry, he called, "I have to go. It was nice meeting you, Harry. Enjoy the movie."

Harry waved, and Randy turned for the door where he paused, speaking softly to his would-have-been date. "We can find another night, but you know what?" He didn't wait for a reply. "You need to decide what you're doing. You're like that guy who spins all the plates on top of sticks on 'The Ed Sullivan Show.' Eventually they're all going to crash. You're not really satisfying anyone this way, including yourself. And you know, I really hate seeing you as David; it just makes everything sort of disgusting. I'll call you."

Jenny stepped out of the bathroom just as the apartment door closed behind Randy.

"What happened?" she asked.

"Randy had to go." David, with Jenny in tow, walked toward the living room. "Let's see how Harry's doing with the schedule."

Harry, however, delivered some bad news. "We've puttzed around too much," he said, "and missed the early show. The next one starts at 10:30."

"That's too late for me." Jenny was disappointed. "I have to work in the morning."

"Well," David offered, "we could see something else. Is there another movie?"

Harry looked through the newspaper. "Not really. I was kind of set on 'Bananas.'"

"It's all right," Jenny interjected, setting her beer down on a table. "You two go to the late show. I should just go home."

Jenny waved to Harry, kissed David, and walked to the door.

"It was good to see you again, Jenny," said Harry. "I had begun to fear you had run off with the departing summer."

David had yet another disgusted and reproachful, but pointless look for his friend.

"Don't see me out," Jenny stopped David. "I'm familiar with the way to the door, even if not, apparently, with your dirty underwear. Call me."

She shut the door behind her and was gone.

"Well," David said resignedly as he sat down, "it's just you and me, Harry. Want another beer?"

"No, I don't think so." Harry stood up, dropping the disheveled newspaper on the floor. "Jenny has the right idea. I've been out running around too much lately. If I'm going to get married, I should become more responsible. I'm going to head out, too."

The apartment door closed behind Harry, as it had behind the others, leaving David alone in his living room. He sat motionless for several minutes, staring at the crumpled newspaper, then took a drink of beer and rose from the chair. Dully, he walked to the bathroom and opened the clothes hamper. Setting the bottle of beer on the sink, he pulled the towels from the top of the pile and extracted, one by one, the items of Lynn's clothing. He held up the little black dress, sadly smoothed it out before putting it on a hanger and taking it, along with the other clothing and the cosmetics case, back to their cabinet.

CHAPTER FOUR

Autumnal Equinox

"Harry," David's patience with his friend had finally exhausted itself, "you've been bugging me about my hair long enough. Could you just let it go?"

Harry was indifferent to the frustration he had caused. "Why don't you grow a long, scruffy beard to go with it," he taunted, "and join all the other Grateful Dead impersonating, druggy Vietnam veterans?"

"That's a cheap shot." David leaned back in the booth and regained his composure. "Not all vets are like that. Most are completely adjusted. It's only a few who haven't gotten on with their lives and are stuck in 1968. They haven't grown up. They'll never get home."

"And you have?"

"I have. I'm aware of where I am. I certainly don't think of the time in Vietnam as the most important thing in my life. I live in the present." He emptied his glass and looked around the corner of the booth for the waitress.

"I meant 'grown up,' not 'come home.'"

"What is that supposed to mean?"

From the pitcher that sat on the table between them, Harry refilled both his own glass and David's. "Nothing. It's just that you're approaching thirty, unmarried, still living in the same apartment you rented when you first got home, and still just barely getting by with this writing thing instead of a real job. You're still going to the same bars." Harry waved an arm about, taking in the entire tavern in which they sat.

"Where do you think you are? And I'm supposed to get married, just because you, amazingly enough, are about to be? You're just trying to drag me along for company on your phony, new-found path of sensibility. And I'm nowhere near thirty."

"No doubt you noticed, David, that over the past few years an increasingly great number of the women I dated prior to finding my true love had been divorced. Doesn't that suggest to you that we have been stagnating, caught in an eddy, that something was passing us by?"

"Yes, it suggests that divorce was passing us by. Find something else to talk about, Harry."

"I don't really have time for a new subject," Harry poured the last drops from the pitcher into his glass." I'm meeting my darling affianced Christine, in a half-hour. What have you on your schedule for the evening?"

"I have a date."

"Aha. A divorcee?"

David, increasingly frustrated with the discussion, barely stifled, "No, he's married," and instead settled for a weak, "No, not a divorcee."

"Jenny?"

"No, not Jenny."

"It seems she was, in spite of your protestations, another summer love."

"Ah, but I do still go out with her occasionally, so there goes your 'season' theory."

"Perhaps. So, where are you going tonight?"

"Just out to dinner somewhere and then hit a bar."

"Well planned. Very mature."

"Shut up, Harry." David finished his beer and, pulling on his jacket, rose to leave. He tossed some money on the table. "I don't see the waitress. Take care of this, will you, and give my regrets to the obviously insane bride-to-be."

Hours later, Lynn eagerly responded to the buzzer announcing a visitor.

"It's Randy," the voice from the lobby announced. "Are you ready?"

"Just. I'll be right down." Lynn ran back to the bathroom, completed packing her purse, and hurried out of the building to find Randy awaiting her beside his two-seater Austin Healey. "You have your own car again," she excitedly observed. "You're not, then returning from a trip?"

"No," Randy held the door open for his date, "tonight I'm attending the company's annual award dinner and trip to the Blackhawks' preseason game, so this restaurant had better be showing the game on TV. I'll have to report."

Lynn settled into the seat in such a way that, as her coat dropped open, her skirt rode up to mid-thigh and she displayed her legs in a manner she hoped Randy would find sexually stimulating. She was pleased to see that he looked furtively out of the corners of his eyes as he drove.

"How long do you have?" she asked.

"Till one, or two, perhaps. Probably no later than that."

"Well," Lynn pondered, "The Hawks will probably be on at the bar, but we may not be able to see it from our table. The "Northwestern Rathskeller" is modeled after a German beer cellar: quiet and dark, and the tables are in little alcoves, but we may be able to get one with a view of the TV."

"I hope we can get in, eat, and get out quickly," Randy said. "Driving all the way downtown and having dinner may not leave us time for 'Charlie's.' We may need to just come back to your place."

"Randy," Lynn placed a hand on his right leg, "I really appreciate your indulgence of this plan. I know you need to use our time to advantage, but I really want to do this. I want to conduct myself more fully in the real world. I will make it up to you."

"It's my pleasure." Randy was magnanimous in his specious endorsement of his lover's scheme.

Lynn leaned back and observed the neighborhoods through which they passed as they drove north to the expressway that would take them downtown.

"Do you mind that we go to 'Charlie's?'" she suddenly and pointedly asked.

"Mind? Don't you want to go there?" Randy gave Lynn a puzzled glance.

"That's not it," she turned in her seat to face him. "It's just that it's pretty much the only place we go. I'm still going to the same bar. Do you ever get tired of it?"

"I thought you enjoyed 'Charlie's.'"

Lynn settled back slouchily in the seat. "I do. I owe it a lot. Most of the gay bars don't really welcome us. Me. People like me. 'Charlie's' has always given us a home. It just seems like it really has no end, no…" she struggled for her meaning, "direction."

Randy considered his date's unexpected mood. "We could just skip it."

"Well, as you say, we may have to, but that's not the point. We're out tonight. Tonight's fine. I think I'd just like to be able to broaden my horizons."

"What would that mean? More time for Lynn?" Randy smiled at his oddly discontented date, then focused on the traffic as he merged onto the expressway, edging into the fast moving stream of cars headed for the city looming bright and tall in the evening sky ahead of them.

"You remember my friend Harry?" Lynn abruptly ended the brief silence. "You met him at my place a while back."

"You've become David. I can't do this if you're David," Randy stated.

"David's friend, Harry," she corrected. "There's a point to this. As loony as Harry is, he's going to get married. He'll become comfortable, surrounded by children and eventually grandchildren. You're the same way. If we stopped doing this, you'd still have a happy, or relatively so, family life. You'd get by. Maybe your wife would even learn to indulge your bondage fantasies. You'd enjoy a healthy family life."

"It hasn't been exactly healthy keeping all this secret."

"But what we do together is not the most important thing in your life. Your kids come first. You'd survive the end of us. I'm going nowhere, though. Not getting straight — oh, ha, ha, that's funny," Lynn chuckled at her unexpected pun, "not fulfilled in either life. Spinning plates, to use your apt simile. David probably couldn't sustain a marriage. He'd blow it over this, and yet this is only part-time."

Unresponsive, Randy concentrated on the road as they drew closer to the city.

"You know what?" Lynn ended the awkward silence, "I wonder if we shouldn't just go back to my place. Just skip the restaurant."

A suggestion of frustration appeared in Randy's tone. "You really wanted to show me this place. We're half-way there."

"What if it's not safe?"

"Not safe?" Randy's glance was not entirely friendly. "It's just blocks from the John Hancock Building. That's a safe neighborhood."

"I don't mean the neighborhood. I mean what if I'm spotted?"

"You won't be. You look more than convincingly female. Besides, you tell me it's a very dark place." Randy directed as much attention to his troubled lover as the traffic would allow. "Lynn," he attempted a reassuring tone, "you won't have any trouble passing. You never do. I have even more to lose than you do and yet I have complete confidence."

"It's getting harder, Randy. Harder to stay thin. I'm getting older. You know, of course that today is the Autumnal Equinox; the sun has left us today, dropped south of the equator."

"What's your point?"

"It's getting darker now. Time is passing, and we're entering a colder season." She paused to think. "I'm not sure I'm getting this across clearly."

"We're all getting older, Lynn. Has David's friend's marriage brought this on?" Randy reached out his right hand and took both of Lynn's in his.

"Maybe so. I guess so." Smiling and apparently dragging herself out of her funk, Lynn slouched even more deeply into the seat. "Forget it. I'll rally."

Soon they approached the massive Central Post Office building towering over the expressway. As the car sped east, Lynn leaned back, watched the expansive face of the edifice loom directly above, then suddenly become a roof as they passed beneath it. Randy edged the car over to the far right lane and, when they emerged from the passage beneath the post office, turned onto an exit ramp requiring a tight two hundred and seventy degree turn and descending beneath the city streets to the cavernous Lower Wacker Drive where traffic, faced with few stop lights, moved swiftly north, then east following beside the Chicago River.

A left turn at the eastern end of Lower Wacker Drive put them onto the bottom level of the Michigan Avenue Bridge, and once across the river, Randy turned right, bringing the car out from the dark underground roadway into the brightly lit, congested streets of the near north side.

"There it is." Lynn pointed to their left after they had crept several blocks in a line of cars filling narrow streets from block end to block end. Bumper to bumper parked cars forced them to drive on past the restaurant and through the succeeding intersection.

As they moved slowly along the next block, a couple walking on the sidewalk caught up with them, passed, and entered a parked car just ahead. Exultant over their good fortune, Randy stopped his car and allowed the departing couple to pull out. Though the larger car had a bit of trouble getting out of the tight space, Randy was able to zip his sports car in, and then he walked around to open the door for Lynn.

Stepping out onto the sidewalk, Lynn watched her legs, concentrated on the feel of her tightening skirt as she placed one and then the other high-heeled shoe onto the pavement. She wrapped her arm around one of Randy's and leaned against him, immersing herself in the feeling of her dress, her man, and the sound of her heels as they walked back to the restaurant. By the time the reached their destination, she felt thoroughly feminine.

The facade of the two-story building, surrounded by lofty steel structures, had been fabricated to simulate a Bavarian chateau. A flight of stairs led to a restaurant on the elevated first floor, but Lynn pulled her date down several flagstone steps to a large wooden door giving access to the cellar. Randy pulled open the heavy door, and the two stepped into a low-ceilinged and, as Lynn had promised, very dimly lit Rathskeller.

They were approached by the *maitre d'* who, after speaking with Randy, led them down a few more steps and past the bar behind which, Randy happily noted, was a television tuned to the Chicago Blackhawks hockey game. Though his attention lingered on the screen, he followed Lynn and their guide into a narrow, vaulted corridor from which there extended, on both sides, successive small alcoves, each containing a rectangular wooden table and two bench seats. Randy halted their progress into this catacomb and asked the *Maitre d'* to seat them in the very first alcove, one that afforded a distant view of the television set.

Lynn gracefully slid onto one of the bench seats, Randy taking the one opposite. He ordered drinks, and after handing them each a menu, the *maitre d'* left them.

Reaching across the table for one of Randy's hands, she pulled his attention back from the hockey game. "See," she said, "I was right, wasn't I? This place is perfect. Quiet and secluded. I'm sorry I was so difficult earlier."

Their waiter delivered a large mug of beer for Randy and a vodka and 7UP for Lynn, promising to return presently to take their order. Lynn took a sip of her drink, then surveyed her surroundings, leaning a bit out of the alcove, but suddenly, with a startled gasp, leaned back in and turned her back to the corridor.

"What's wrong?" Randy asked.

"Look," Lynn whispered. "No," she reached across the table to stop Randy from looking out of their alcove, "I mean don't look. The girl at the table across from us. It's Jenny. You remember her. You met her at my apartment a while back. She's out with another man."

"So what?" Randy displayed disinterest. "So are you."

"That's not the point. I introduced her to this place. Now she brings someone else here."

"And you're upset? I thought you had backed off from that relationship. Oof, bad goal." Randy's focus was clearly on the television. "This sucks, Lynn." He turned back to his date.

"What? Who scored?"

"Not the game. You. Once again you've turned into David. I'm not out here to have sex with another man."

"You're right, Randy. I'm sorry. I just hope she doesn't recognize me."

"She's not going to recognize you." Randy glanced over at the other table. "She's obviously caught up in her date. You certainly seem to have these ridiculous coincidences a lot."

Lynn tugged at her skirt, repositioned her feet, and closed her eyes, seeking to reach back into her femininity. She looked down at her bodice, breathed in and out, watching her breasts rise, and finally smiled across the table.

"I'm fine." She thrust the toe of her shoe into Randy's pant cuff. "Let's order."

Randy attracted the attention of the waiter and ordered dinner. As they waited for their food, they spoke little, Randy's attention regularly distracted by the hockey game on which he would have to report. Just as the waiter arrived with their food, Lynn saw Jenny and her date rise to leave. They passed out of the narrow hallway without a look into their neighbors' alcove, and, though she did not allude to it, Lynn experienced considerable relief.

Their own meal finished, Randy and Lynn enjoyed a final round of drinks, during which time Lynn slipped Randy some money to cover her portion of the bill. Leaving the restaurant, they passed the bar, and Randy pointed out that the game was disastrous, the Blackhawks down by four goals in the last period, and that he, then, would be able to just disgustedly dismiss it without the need to recount specifics.

"It's only a preseason game," he rationalized.

Back in the car, before pulling out of the parking space, Randy asked Lynn if she wanted to go to 'Charlie's'.

"No," she answered after a brief consideration. "I've really spoiled much of tonight for you. Let's just go to my place, and I'll do my best to make amends. I did stop being me. Sometimes I just lose focus. It happens when I'm David with a girl, and tonight it happened to Lynn."

"It's happening again."

"Yes, it is. You're right. I've got to get better at this."

They drove back out of the downtown in silence, but when they were comfortably cruising west along the Eisenhower Expressway toward the suburbs, Randy expressed his concerns.

"Listen," he suddenly began, "this is important. The whole premise of our relationship is that you're female. I'm not gay, and when you're male, it makes me very uncomfortable. We seem to be having some difficulty maintaining the barriers."

"And yet," realizing that she could be treading close to a line between discussion and confrontation and desiring to avoid crossing that line, Lynn paused and formed her response carefully, "if I were a genetic woman, that wouldn't work for your marital fidelity rationale." She hoped to stay safely within lighthearted irony.

"Yes," Randy answered. "That doesn't really make much sense, does it? It's kind of delusional."

"No more so, I guess, than convincing myself that sex with females when I am male and with males when female both constitute heterosexuality."

Again they settled into a silence. Some miles passed, and Lynn snuggled close to Randy.

"You're right," she said. "It is time to poop or get off the pot."

"Some more unladylike profanity." Randy smiled at the woman leaning onto his shoulder.

"I mean it. I'm going to show you. I will not fail again, because I will work to eliminate the flip-flops. Lynn is taking over, and she begins tonight. I've actually been giving this a lot of thought for some time.

Before we met, Randy, I used to just put on women's clothes, have an orgasm, and take them off. Then I started going out – to 'Charlie's' – and spending hours as Lynn. We met, and it became clear that I want to truly experience being a woman, but still, it was mostly about sex."

"And now that's not the case?" Randy rather mockingly inquired.

"Sex is still important," Lynn smiled at her lover, "but now there's more. Do you know what I've discovered since I started shaving and being me even in the warm months?"

"No."

"The clothes are not for sex. I don't want to put on the clothes just to be aroused, I want to wear them because it's natural to do so. The proper thing. All the time. I want to wake up in the morning and just naturally get dressed. Do you have any idea how exiting a brassiere is?"

"Yes, actually, I do."

"That's not what I mean, Randy. I mean how exciting it is that a bra is a casual, natural thing to have on. I want putting one on to be as ordinary as it is when you put on your socks. The rush is that there is no rush. It's not a fetish, it's an article of clothing, and I want it to be an article of clothing I wear because of who I am. Lynn. Me."

Lynn stopped, and Randy apparently had no idea what to say.

Having articulated this evolving conviction, Lynn, obviously energized, leaned against Randy's body, put her hand back on his leg, and rode in contented silence the rest of the trip to her home.

Several hours later in Lynn's bed, Randy suddenly sat up and reached for her alarm clock. "It's one A. M.," he announced. "I've got to get going."

He gathered his clothes from the floor and hurriedly dressed. As he sat on the bed to tie his shoes, he turned to Lynn who lay beside him, and untied the rope that bound her ankles. With a bit of struggle, she was able to put her feet on the floor and sit up on the edge of the bed.

"Sorry to be so abrupt," Randy said, standing to buckle his belt. "I really have to hustle, though." He helped Lynn to stand, then turned her and untied her wrists.

"It was wonderful, Randy," Lynn said. "To coin a phrase, you made me feel like a natural woman."

"You don't need to see me to the door," Randy kissed her, then ran out of the bedroom and down the hall.

When she had heard the apartment door slam shut, Lynn kicked off her shoes and undressed. From her dresser drawer she took a long, satin nightgown, its location in the dresser testifying to Lynn's commitment to living as nearly full-time as possible. She dropped the nightgown over her head and wiggled fully into it, then went to the bathroom, washed, brushed her teeth, and went to bed.

Only moments had elapsed, though, before she sat up, turned on her light, and went to her closet cabinet. Rummaging about its floor, she found a purse she had not used for some months and dug through it until she retrieved the therapist's business card Jeannie had given her.

She placed the card on the table beside he bed where it would be available in the morning and then contentedly lay down to sleep.

CHAPTER FIVE

Winter Solstice

1.

Three days before Christmas, 1971, Lynn intended to celebrate the third anniversary of David Stewart's return home from Vietnam with an evening of adventure and a night of sensual pleasure. As the setting winter solstice sun, closing the shortest day of the year, was quietly withdrawing its slanting light from the interior of her apartment, she stood before the hallway mirror wearing a long-sleeved, tight black dress, a bit more low-cut than she was used to, and knee-high, black high-heeled boots. She was exceptionally pleased with her appearance, particularly with the length of her hair, now cascading well below her shoulders, but the ring of her telephone interrupted her assessment, drawing her reluctantly away from the mirror to the golden, hazy sunset of the living room. Unhesitatingly, without concern for who the caller might be, she answered in a practiced female voice.

"Lynn, it's Randy. We're on a break, but I'll be done with this presentation in about two more hours. Can I assume you still want to meet at this bar you've picked?"

"Indeed, you can." Lynn conveyed joyful buoyancy. "I'm just about to leave for the train station."

"Train station? You're taking a train?"

"And then a bus. I've planned it all out." Lynn smiled with anticipation and excitement. "I'm not sneaking into the city in my car tonight. I'm riding public transportation like any other young woman would. Don't you think I can do it?"

"I have every confidence in you, Lynn. You're a beautiful woman. The only attention you will draw will be admiration. I'll see you at the bar."

Lynn hung up the phone and walked to the sliding glass door giving access to the balcony of her second floor apartment. The final few minutes of sunlight cast a golden hue in the sky and glistened across the snow-covered quadrangle below. Surrounded by buildings identical to her own, the park was empty and silent. Lynn shifted her focus to her own reflection in the glass door and resumed appreciative study of her appearance.

"Legs look great," she concluded, studying the effect of the boots and the short hemline of her dress. She walked well, she believed, comfortably with a fluid, feminine gracefulness. She grabbed her coat from the sofa where it lay with her purse and gloves, put it on and tightly cinched its belt. The coat was short, reaching just to the length of her dress, and Lynn was pleased that it allowed exposure of her legs and boots. She pulled on her faux leather gloves, a particularly sensual addition, and checked through her purse to confirm the ready availability of her train ticket and the exact change for the bus she would be taking from Chicago's Union Station.

Satisfied, she placed the purse over her shoulder and moved toward the apartment door. She had prepared and left on the kitchen table an overnight bag with an emergency supply of male clothing, but, as she passed the kitchen, she looked in and rejected the idea of taking it.

"No," she reflected, "I'm a woman. I have no need for that."

Without further hesitation she stepped out of her apartment and along the hall to the stairway.

A light snow had fallen earlier in the day, adding itself to the season's rather modest accumulation, but Lynn was able to follow a shoveled walk beyond her unit and past another, turning right on the sidewalk beside a street leading toward the train station. There was no traffic moving on the street beside her, and as she passed the several apartment buildings facing the street, she was able, in the waning evening light, to watch her reflections in the patio doors of the successive apartments. The image presented was of an attractive woman, and she was greatly encouraged. As she approached a walk leading to the entrance of the last building of her complex, though, its door opened and a man emerged. Startled, Lynn feared appearing nervous, but the man simply smiled at her as they passed each other. She walked on, tense, waiting for some alarm of recognition, but none came.

"First test," she thought. "Passed." But then she comprehended what she had done. She had been a male in woman's clothing fearing discovery.

"Last time," she told herself. "There is nothing to discover. I am just as I ought to be."

A hundred yards ahead of her the street intersected with 55th Street, a major east-west roadway through several of Chicago's western suburbs. Reaching the intersection and waiting for the light to change and allow her to cross, she confidently watched the passing cars, feeling no need to maintain any sort of lowered profile. The light changed, traffic halted, and she stepped from the curb, walking breezily and exchanging flirtatious smiles with the young male driver of the lead car to her right.

Having reached the other sidewalk, she heard the traffic resume its passage behind her and found herself regretting that she was no longer the sole interesting sight for so many waiting and weary commuters.

North of 55th Street the nature of Lynn's hometown is dramatically different. The northern part is old, older by a hundred years than the apartment complexes and mini-malls that have supplanted cornfields south of that roadway, and having put that intersection behind her, she no longer followed a wide, straight street, but rather navigated a sidewalk following beside a narrow, curving road embracing the gentle rise and fall of the land, a road surveyed by planners who envisioned beauty in forms other than sterile grids.

She passed stately homes set far back from the sidewalk on expansive lawns meticulously landscaped beneath towering oak, maple, and elm trees. The neighborhood was silent; neither pedestrians nor automobiles disturbed the snow-softened winter evening peace.

Crumbled sidewalks tumbling over assertive tree roots, however, harbored patches of unshoveled snow and ice and made walking in high heels more precarious. Lynn had to slow her pace, and when she crested a rise beyond which she could see the town's business district and the train station, she heard the crossing bells sound, announcing an approaching train, and she saw the gates begin to descend.

Fearing missing her train, she hurried past the final home at the edge of the commercial district and was able to walk more quickly on the smoother, cleared sidewalks fronting the block of upscale shops. The train hooted across the town's main street and gasped to a stop at the station. Few people disembarked, and still fewer waited to board. The train's time at the station would be short.

When she reached the depot parking lot, Lynn observed the two conductors assist the final boarding passenger onto the train and step up from the platform to the railcar steps and she began to run. One of the conductors, hanging onto the doorway's center pole, leaned out to signal the engineer to depart, but before giving the wave that would leave Lynn at the station, he glanced across the parking lot and spotted the frantic, late arriving passenger. He dropped back down to the platform and waited, interestedly watching Lynn's progress. Assured, then, that she would catch the train, Lynn felt exhilaration, hoping that the two conductors were enjoying the sight of a woman running in high-heeled boots and a tight skirt.

Reaching the boarding platform, she slowed to a walk. The blue-suited trainmen smiled as she arrived and greeted her, addressing her as, "Miss." The one on the platform took her elbow and the other on the train reached down to aid her up the steps and into the vestibule between compartments where, safely aboard, Lynn allowed herself to retrospectively savor the thrill of her successful run in female clothing and the attention of the conductors.

She slid open the door leading to the forward compartment and turned immediately to climb the winding staircase leading to the train car's left side upper deck where a narrow aisle gave access to a row of single seats, chosen for the fact that they precluded the possibility of conversation with a seat-mate.

As the train pulled out of the station, she selected a seat and extracted from her purse her ticket and a book. Leaning down to her right, she slid the ticket into a clip from which the conductor, walking the center aisle below, would be able to administer his official punch. The book, more prop than sincere interest, she placed on her lap for later use. Subtly surveying the interior of the car, she noticed a man seated on the right side upper deck. He was looking directly at her and did not avert his gaze when she locked eyes with him. She smiled and he smiled back, but desiring no escalation of interest, she opened and affected interest in her book.

The train accelerated past the backyards of costly homes and achieved a stable speed that lasted only a few moments before the brakes were applied for a stop in another quiet suburb. The pattern repeated through several towns, each unique, but all sharing a satisfied upper-middle class sheen. When the train crossed east beyond Harlem Avenue, though, it entered a starkly differing community. Looking up from her book, Lynn observed considerably smaller backyards, more modest homes. Drawing close to the city, the train began to pass through dirtier, grittier, working class neighborhoods of bungalows crowded within a few feet of each other and duplexes scattered among factories and warehouses.

Both the upper classes and the sun faded in the train's wake. Dusk and finally full darkness asserted themselves in turn over the world outside Lynn's window, and as they did, she discovered something of interest. Though she could still just make out the buildings alternating with garishly lit intersections past which the train continued on its final, uninterrupted run to the city, she could refocus her eyes and see in the glass the reflection of the car's interior and that of the man seated opposite her. He was reading a newspaper, apparently no longer interested in her.

With a mixture of relief and incompletely suppressed disappointment, she returned her attention to the book and passed the last minutes of the trip comfortably lost in its pages.

A long, slowing, grating turn to the north signaled approach to Union Station, and though the car began to sway and wobble across the many switches, the people in the seats below Lynn gathered their belongings and filed to the rear of the car, preparing to disembark as soon as the train halted.

The several passengers in the upper decks, two on Lynn's side and three, including the briefly appreciative man, on the other, also began to fold up newspapers and secure their bags and coats, and when the train's air brakes exuded their final gasp, bringing the train to a halt in the storied depot, Lynn rose and made her way, last of all, along the narrow aisle. Halfway down the winding stairs she caught up with the two others from her deck waiting for a chance to merge into the flow of main floor passengers pushing through the doorway to the vestibule.

As they moved forward and Lynn eased down the staircase and around its turn to face the stairs from the opposite deck, she confronted the man with whom she had exchanged smiles. The press of humanity, though, commanded his attention, and he stepped into the flow and was gone. Lynn had little opportunity to consider her feelings about being so casually unconsidered. Seeking an opportunity to step down among the people moving through the doorway, she encountered a young mother herding two small children toward the exit. The woman returned Lynn's smile and pulled back on her children's shoulders, offering a Lynn a chance to join the flow.

Hesitant to speak to thank the woman, Lynn attempted to convey gratitude with a nod and smile, vaguely troubled by a fear that another woman might prove more perceptive than men. She stepped down into the mass of people, moved out to the vestibule and down the steps leading to the platform. There were no conductors to offer aid, so with some trepidation she grabbed the vertical bar in the center of the stairway and made the large step down. Her dress pulled tight, but in spite of that and of her high heels, she stepped firmly onto the concrete.

Feeling a bit of excitement from the pull of her dress, she turned left and assumed the pace of the massing crowd moving quickly toward the terminal. Though she immediately sought to push the thought out of her consciousness, she momentarily reflected on her successful close interaction with another woman. She enjoyed the sound of her heels on the pavement and, walking with the crowd along the platform between parked trains, immersed herself more deeply into the pleasant sensation of walking as a woman among people who accepted her as such.

The portion of Union Station entered by the arriving passengers had once been a vast and cavernous depot, but had, in the name of progress, surrendered its air space to a towering office building and been transformed into an unprepossessing basement filled with snack bars, magazine counters, and stairways. Once inside this, the crowd dispersed, heading for myriad destinations served by various exits. Lynn knew her route and moved quickly toward a corridor leading beneath Canal Street to the historic part of the station that had thankfully been spared progress.

Rounding the corner of a newsstand, she encountered a group of teenage boys sitting in wait on their luggage, and clearly they noticed her. She experienced a slight, involuntary panic, but averted her gaze and strode on.

"Ooh, la, la," the call obviously directed at her followed.

"Ooh, la, la?" she thought. "Is he kidding? Does he mean it?" She worried that the youths may have perceived the truth, but no more outbursts trailed after her. "So it seems to have been sincere," she determined, "corny, but sincere," and she smiled with satisfaction. How wonderful to be the object of appreciative male attention. She circled around a hot dog kiosk and entered the wide tunnel that passes beneath the street and leads to the vast, vaulted landmark Union Station waiting room through which she longed to walk as a woman.

The tunnel led her past a row of ticket sales windows on her left and on her right, a large snack bar. Though ticket buyers were lined up at the several windows, few people were moving through the tunnel; Lynn had a wide space in which to walk, and she fully engaged the opportunity.

Her comfort was jeopardized, though, when a Chicago policeman, munching a hamburger, stepped out of the snack bar to her right and walked directly toward her. As it was too late to change course, Lynn steeled herself to brazen it out, to do nothing to betray her fear or to draw attention to herself. The policeman stuffed the last of the burger into his mouth, tossed the wrapper into a trash bin, and, relieved of that concern, surveyed his surroundings, the most prominent element of which was the woman whose pathway was about to intersect his own. As they came along side each other, the officer nodded a friendly greeting and passed on. No arrest. No interrogation. Lynn perceptibly sagged with relief; the policeman had bought it. If she could pass that test, she could pass any but the ultimate.

Buoyed, confident, she lengthened her stride just a bit, subtly increased the swing of her hips, placing each step just a bit more fully on the axis of her path. Careful to avoid ludicrous exaggeration, she was indeed a woman walking in public and attracting the admiration of men she passed. It became intoxicating.

Her continued progress to the waiting room brought her close to the ticket lines. At the back end of one stood a tall, perhaps six-three, lanky soldier waiting patiently beside his duffle bag. The patch he wore on his dress green uniform caught Lynn's attention: it was the patch of the unit in which David had served in Vietnam, and, as had David, the soldier wore sergeant's stripes below it and a Combat Infantry Badge above his left breast pocket.

Lynn veered a bit to approach him more closely, studying him intently. Obviously he was just returning home. As she drew near, the soldier turned and looked directly at her. His eyes grew wide in apparent amazement.

"You're beautiful," he said with a humbled awe that Lynn remembered from David's first days back in country.

Surprised, she smiled at the soldier, who took a step closer.

"Merry Christmas," he simply offered, conveying childlike wonder in his expressive, youthful face.

Lynn, excitedly flattered, continued on a few steps past her well-wisher, then stopped. She turned back, studied again the patch on his shoulder and the ribbons on his chest, then approached him and, reaching up with a gloved hand to touch his cheek, quickly kissed him, and just as quickly did an about face to continue on her way.

Her impulsive act elicited appreciative hoots and whistles from the commuters in the various ticket lines, but she did not look back. The excitement behind her gradually subsided, and soon she emerged from the tunnel into the stunning, immense waiting room stretching out before her to the right and left and looming stories above to an ornate, vaulted ceiling. She looked up and about at the classic statuary adorning the upper reaches of the walls and stopped to take in the incredible scale of space that reduced the substantial wooden benches lined up throughout the expansive room to seeming miniatures.

Lynn had intended this to be the highlight of her adventure. She had long imagined listening to her high heels ring against the tile floor and echo through the vastness and had planned to linger over the intense opportunity to walk about that tremendous space in a dress, but some commotion back in the tunnel drew her attention. She saw that the soldier had hoisted his duffle onto his shoulder and, with the raucous encouragement of his ticket-line mates, started off in her direction. The kiss had been a mistake. She could not allow him to catch up, so she forgot the statues and the columns and her plans and set off quickly for the wide stone staircase leading up to Canal Street. Her flight took her out of the soldier's view, but again unwisely she paused at the foot of the stairs to look back and she saw him emerge from the tunnel, spot her, and begin to run after her.

She walked rapidly up the first few stairs, but as soon as she was again out of the soldier's line of vision, ran up the rest. The climb was long, and at the top, just before pushing through the glass door to the street, Lynn again looked back. Far below, her pursuer, with the strength and stamina of a combat soldier, was taking the steps two at a time, apparently unhampered by the weight of his duffle.

Lynn's route planning and some good fortune served her well. Just across the sidewalk outside the door the bus she needed, the 151 route, was about to pull away. The bus' door was hissing shut, and the driver was releasing the brakes, but she ran the few steps to the curb and pounded on the closing door. To her relief, the driver decided to let her on, reopened the door, and she climbed up the steps, fumbling in her purse for the preset proper change, which she dropped into the hopper. She moved swiftly down the aisle, lurching a bit as the bus pulled out from the stop, and when she found an unoccupied seat she sat down and slid across to the window.

The pursuing sergeant burst out onto the sidewalk and searched frantically in both directions. Frustrated, he looked up at the departing bus and when he spotted Lynn watching him from one of its windows, he visibly drooped with disappointment, dropping his duffle onto the pavement.

Lynn raised a hand in an uncertain, apologetic wave, but the soldier did not respond; he just watched as the bus reached the corner and turned left into the eastbound traffic on Jackson Boulevard.

Relieved at her escape, yet somewhat saddened, Lynn turned her face from the window and, pulling her book from her purse, settled in for a rather long ride. The bus threaded its way across Chicago's "Loop" to State Street, turned north, eventually reaching Inner Lake Shore Drive where, free of stop signs and cross streets, it picked up speed.

She had devoured several chapters when the bus bounced through a sizeable pothole, jostling her and interrupting her concentration. Leaning against the bulkhead of the bus, she strained to look through the reflecting window into the darkness outside. As the bus drove through a bright cone of streetlamp illumination, she caught a glimpse of a sign that read "Addison Street." Addison Street. She had intended to get off at Belmont Avenue. She was at least six blocks north of her stop and traveling fast. She reached above the window and pulled the cord, signaling the driver that she wished to get off at the next stop, then rose and, hanging on to the vertical standee poles, made her way to the exit. Moments later the bus came to a halt, and the pneumatic door fooshed open.

Lynn stepped down, and the bus pulled away, leaving her alone on a concrete island at the edge of Lake Shore Drive, standing illuminated in the darkness by the glaring, sterile spotlight of an overhead streetlamp. Barely inches away, separated by a chain link fence, the southbound traffic of the Outer Drive zoomed past. In the other direction she looked across two lanes of traffic to the safety of a sidewalk and rows of north shore apartment buildings.

She looked both directions, waited for a sufficient break in the more slowly moving Inner Drive traffic, then ran across the roadway, reaching the curb without incident. Choosing a quiet east-west street, she walked west, calculating the distance to the bar where she was to meet Randy: two blocks west to Broadway, then about six blocks south. Farther to walk than she had intended, but the neighborhood, though dark, was affluent and safe, and she decided to enjoy the opportunity.

By the time she closed to within a block of her destination - a North Broadway gay bar offering cover for herself in the unfortunate event of discovery and possessing a prominently advertised and popular straight-welcoming policy that would provide some comfort for Randy - the pleasures of her trek had succumbed to a growing discomfort in her feet and toes, and when she reached the tavern, she was anxious to locate Randy and a place to sit. The former wish was immediately met, as she found her lover, greatly distressed by his surroundings, standing just inside the doorway.

"At last." Randy immediately and theatrically embraced her. "I was beginning to worry. There have been a couple guys giving me the sideways eye. I thought I'd have to wait outside. Did you have some trouble?"

"Not really," Lynn leaned against him. "I'll tell you all about it, but I really need a place to sit down."

Though the early evening darkness of the season suggested otherwise, the night was young, and the Monday crowd sparse, so when the two lovers had made their way to the rear of the room, Randy emphasizing his heterosexual identity by keeping an arm firmly wrapped around Lynn's shoulders, they readily found a vacant table. When Randy had helped her remove her coat, Lynn happily plopped into a chair.

"That's a relief," she sighed. "Could you get me a drink, and then I'll relate my adventures."

By the time Randy returned with a beer and Lynn's standard Vodka and 7-Up, she was considerably revived. She sat up straight, took a long and satisfying drink, and then began to recount the story of her travels.

"First," she began, "I nearly missed the train and then failed to pay attention on the bus, missed my stop, rode all the way to Addison, and had to walk back. But," she warmed to the next part of her tale, "in Union Station some young guys called out, `Oo-la-la,' as I walked past, and they were serious."

"Oo-la-la?" Randy was incredulous. "People haven't said, `Oo-a-la,' for several centuries."

"They did tonight. It was great, but that's not the best part. As I walked over to the waiting room, I passed a soldier waiting at the back of the line to buy a ticket on the suburban line. He had been in the same unit as David. He had a combat infantry badge, and was probably just getting home from Vietnam." She paused for a more genteel sip of her drink. "Anyway, he sort of stared at me and as I was walking by, he said, 'You're beautiful,' and he wished me a Merry Christmas."

"That's very nice." Randy was unimpressed.

"No, wait. After he wished me Merry Christmas, I kissed him."

This latter revelation made an impression. "You kissed him?"

"Right smack on the lips. You should have heard the crowd in line; they were hooting and whistling."

"I'm not so sure that was a good idea."

"Actually," Lynn leaned back, "it almost wasn't. He picked up his duffle bag and took off after me as I went to the bus stop. I barely made it to a bus that was just pulling out. I felt kind of bad, seeing him watch the bus depart with me on it. But, isn't that kind of neat?"

Randy pondered for a few moments. "It really wasn't a good idea, Lynn. I don't wish to allude to that which we ignore, but I know everything; that soldier doesn't. You can get yourself into a dangerous situation fooling with guys who don't know."

"Yes, I know that's true," Lynn conceded. "I've heard some stories at 'Charlie's' of girls who've been beaten up because they tried to fool some unsuspecting straight guy, but really, it seemed that the poor sergeant should be welcomed home on this happiest day of the year."

"Happiest day of the year?"

"Certainly. Remember in September when I reported that the sun was leaving? Well today it begins to return to our half of the planet. Each day gets sunnier. The dark no longer reigns triumphant."

"Very poetic, but I need another beer. I'd like to get going after that, though. I've got to get up early tomorrow to drive out to my in-laws and catch up with the family.

"You're staying there for the holidays?"

"No," Randy rose to head to the bar, and while he paused to explain, took Lynn's empty glass. "We'll all drive back home Christmas Eve."

"You know," Randy began when he had returned with the drinks. "I'm not sure I understand the point of this whole operation. We're just going to drive to your place; why didn't you just wait for me there? Why take a train and a bus just to turn around and go back?"

"Randy," Lynn leaned across the table and took his hand, "the train and bus journeys were just part of the larger one – ooh, I am poetic, am I not – the larger journey on which you've launched me. The trip was the point, not a means. I'm learning to move about in the real world."

"Well, when you're ready to move about in the real world some more, let me know, and we'll take off. I feel a bit awkward here."

"Empathetic as ever, Randy."

A rather ridiculous, exaggerated smile and a beer glass raised in salute were all Lynn received in response to her sarcasm.

Randy soon finished that glass of beer, and, sympathetic to his desire to depart, Lynn quickly finished her drink and stood up, handing her coat to her date, who helped her on with it. Having put on his own jacket, Randy, careful to demonstrate his attachment to a woman, escorted his date out of the tavern.

2.

Early the next evening Lynn, dressed in athletic shorts and a sports bra, was feverishly pushing her way through a set of sit-ups on her living room floor when the ringing telephone frustrated her count. She jumped to her feet and ran for the phone, answering with a panting, strained voice.

"Lynn?" The caller was clearly uncertain.

"Randy!" Lynn responded with surprise. I didn't expect to hear from you for a couple weeks."

Speaking in a near whisper, Randy nonetheless conveyed some urgency. "That didn't sound like you."

"I was exercising."

"Ah," Randy moved right on to the matter of his call. "Have you read today's 'Tribune'?"

"The 'Tribune?' No. I thought you were at your in-laws."

"I am. We…"

"You read the paper even at your in-laws?" Lynn interrupted.

Though his voice was still a whisper, it conveyed a considerable amount of frustration. "Will you let me speak? I have to be quick. Your soldier is looking for you. He took out an ad in today's personals."

"You read the personals?"

"Focus, Lynn. I told you fooling with the unsuspecting was unwise. He's attempting to find you."

"Well, he can't find me just by taking out a personal ad. We're not in a Sherlock Holmes story. How could he have taken out an ad in one day?"

"Who knows. Maybe he went right over to the Tribune Tower after you ditched him, and they took pity on the returning soldier. I can't talk anymore. I've got to go. Just be a bit less irresponsible. I'll call after the holidays. Merry Christmas, as the soldiers apparently say."

Randy unceremoniously hung up, and Lynn walked to her couch and sat, looking through her glass patio door at the snow gently falling through the darkness. She pondered the information Randy had related, considered the merits of his advice, and relived the thrill she had experienced kissing the soldier.

Resolved, she abruptly rose from the couch and ran to her bedroom. She pulled on some sweatpants and a bulky sweatshirt, pulled her hair into a ponytail, and, regretting the necessity to revert to David, changed her shoes for a pair of his. David grabbed his wallet from a dresser drawer, then ran back along the hallway to the coat closet to get a jacket. Soon he was out the apartment door and down the hallway and staircase at the bottom of which he did a 180 and ran out the building's back door into the central courtyard. As he ran, his footprints marred the unblemished snowfall, leaving a single trail across the park and between the two buildings comprising the north side of the apartment complex. He crossed the parking lot behind those buildings and ducked through a gap in a tall hedgerow, emerging in the brightly lit parking lot of a Jewel Food Store.

Hustling against the cold, he pushed through the slowly opening automatic door and walked directly to the newspaper rack where he picked up a copy of the "Chicago Tribune." Continuing to move swiftly, with predetermined purpose, he collected a six pack of beer from the liquor department, made his purchases, and retraced his steps, leaving the evidence of his return to his apartment in the courtyard snow.

Once inside, David dumped his coat on the floor and the newspaper and six pack on the kitchen table, pulling out and opening one of the bottles. He quickly lost the sweatpants and shirt and David's shoes.

With her hair again freed from the ponytail, Lynn snatched up the newspaper, sat on her sofa, and spread "The Tribune" out on the coffee table. A few minutes of searching discovered the ad, which read: "Seeking the woman who gave a returning soldier a kiss Monday evening in Union Station. Must meet you. Please respond to this paper," and it listed a response code. He had signed it, "Sergeant in Love."

Lynn sat back and drank from her beer, read the ad again, and slouched back deeply in the sofa. When she was ready for a second beer, she returned to her kitchen and poured this one into a glass. She dug some unused and uncrumpled notebook paper out of the cluttered stack of writings and carefully penned a response to be submitted to the paper for the "Sergeant in Love."

3.

Early Saturday night, two days after Christmas, Lynn stepped from the cold of Chicago's northern suburbs into the darkened warmth of "Charlie's," hung her coat on the rack in the vestibule, and took a seat at the nearly empty bar.

"On your own tonight, Hon?" Barry asked as he placed a coaster before his new customer.

"Yes, Barry, I am. And it seems I'm not exactly in a crowd here tonight."

"You always say that, and I always point out that it's early. It's Saturday, so it should pick up. Generally the weather doesn't discourage our population from a chance for a night out. Vodka and Seven-Up?"

When Barry returned with Lynn's drink, he pulled over a stool and sat down.

"Mind a chat? I seem to have the opportunity right now. Is Randy coming in?"

"No," Lynn answered, "It's pretty much family time for him through the holidays."

"Did you have a Merry Christmas?"

"Yes, I did. I went home to my parents for a couple days, and that was fun, if rather stifling. The hormones are beginning to make hiding Lynn a bit difficult."

"So you're really moving along, then?" Barry asked.

"Yes, I'm living female almost full time now, and there are some aspects of life that are becoming a bit awkward. Remember that girl Margie you told me about? Randy's previous ...something. You said she moved to New York for a clean start. I've been giving that some thought. It would make living as Lynn a bit easier; no David friends to intrude or require inconvenient switches."

"That's a big step. How does Randy feel about it?"

Lynn thought for a moment. "That's not really an issue. My departure would just be an inconvenience."

"That sounds a bit cold."

"It's not, though. We both understand our roles. I'm just a sideshow for Randy, an accommodation for his special interest."

"And he for you?"

Again Lynn took a moment to consider her answer. "There's no emotional attachment. Randy – actually, I guess men in general – are the means for me to be female. There would seem to be little else that would be as effective in making one feel a woman as to be with a man. Does that sound selfish?"

Barry merely shrugged.

"What's more," Lynn continued, "Randy has pointed out that balancing two lives has often been less than successful, so it's sort of his impetus." A sudden thought allowed her to turn the conversation to something less ponderous. She sat eagerly forward, leaning across the bar. "But enough of that. Let me tell you about this thing that happened to me just before Christmas."

Barry glanced around the bar and, satisfied his offices were still unrequired, offered Lynn his rapt attention.

"Randy's family went to the grandparents Monday," Lynn began, "but he had to stay in town to do a presentation for a client in the city, so he wasn't going to join them until the next day, so we had a night and arranged to meet at "The Grotto" on Broadway when he'd completed his presentation."

"'The Grotto.' Well. How unloyal." Barry exaggerated an indignant response.

Caught up in her story, Lynn ignored the bartender's comment. "I wanted to travel downtown on public transportation - a big step in my progress - so I took the train in to the city and a bus up to the north side. When I was walking through Union Station some young guy hollered, 'Oo-la-la,' at me."

"'Oo-la-la?' Are you sure he was a young guy, not some octogenarian."

"That's sort of what Randy thought, but no, he was young. 'Oo-la-la' is pretty cool, though. So then I had to walk past a cop, and he just smiled and went on his way, and then I saw a soldier, apparently just back from Vietnam, in line to buy a suburban train ticket, and he told me I was beautiful and wished me a Merry Christmas."

"Seems appropriate."

"But then," Lynn drew Barry in, "I kissed him." She sat back to accept his appreciation, but the bartender said nothing, adopted a scowling, critical expression.

Lynn embellished. "The people in line went wild, whistling and hollering. It was great."

Barry, though, failed to share her joy. "I'm not so sure that sort of thing is wise, Lynn," he said. "Girls have been beaten up when they've tried to fool straight guys."

Lynn was disappointed. "That's pretty much what Randy said, but it was all right. The soldier had no clue. He actually tried to follow me, but I got on the bus before he could catch up."

"Well, that's good. I'm glad nothing more came of it." Another quick assessment of his customers, or lack thereof, assured him that he could prolong the conversation.

"Well," overcoming a hesitation, in the light of Barry's unsympathetic reaction to her story, Lynn continued, "it seems he's trying to find me. He took out an ad in the 'Tribune' personal columns asking me to write and identify myself."

"The personal columns? I didn't think anyone read those, let alone answered them."

"Sometimes people do."

Barry picked up on the implication. "You answered the ad?"

"Sort of."

"Sort of? How can you sort of answer an ad? What did you do?"

"I sent a note to the mailbox he listed."

"You told him the truth, I hope."

"Not exactly."

Barry placed his elbows on the bar and held his head in his hands.

Lynn attempted to defend herself. "He's just back from Vietnam, Barry. I know what that's like. He deserves some consideration."

"What consideration did you give him?"

"My phone number."

Barry stood up and confronted Lynn with a serious and earnest appeal. "Lynn, you can't fool straight guys this way. I'm serious about girls getting smacked around. And as you say, this guy's just back from a combat zone. He's liable to freak out."

"Well, he may never call."

A customer, bearing an empty glass, walked up to the other side of the bar, and as Barry stepped away, he offered a parting shot. "If he does, you've got to cut it off right away. Tell him the truth, or give some other reason for never meeting him. Promise me."

The bartender turned away too quickly to notice that Lynn offered no assent to his request for a promise.

Gradually, Barry's prediction that the evening would grow more active once again proved true, and it was some time before he was able to return and serve Lynn another drink. Neither of them, though, alluded to their previous topic; instead Barry inquired about her plans for New Year's Eve.

"I'll be here," she eagerly reported. "I've got a great new dress and some long formal gloves I haven't had an excuse to wear for a while. I'm looking forward to it. And then Jeannie's having a party after 'Charlie's' closes."

"And Randy will be with his family."

"That's correct," she confirmed. "He's completely unavailable for the holidays, but alone or with a date, this is the prime spot for a girl like me that night."

In the late afternoon of New Year's Eve, in spite of the cold, Lynn completed a long run, and just as she returned to her apartment, leaning back exhaustedly against the door to shut it, she heard the phone ring. Somewhat out of breath, she forgot herself and answered the call with an errant maleness.

"This is Andy Johnson," an obviously puzzled voice responded. "I'm calling for Lynn."

Caught completely by surprise, Lynn reacted with stunned silence.

"Sir?" the caller tried again.

She looked about in confusion, then said, "Lynn. Yes, Lynn is here. Just a moment while I get her." She set the receiver down on the table with an exaggerated clunk and took a few steps away. A bit panicked, she quickly pondered a course of action, then, with a deep breath to relax, walked back to the phone.

"This is Lynn," her regrouping allowed return of her feminine voice. Clearly some level of excitement reigned at the other end.

"Lynn, this is Sergeant, or rather officially now, former Sergeant Andy Johnson. From the train station?" A lack of response caused the former soldier some uncertainty. "You sent me a letter, told me to call this number."

Again there was some hesitation before she spoke, but Lynn was able to muster sufficient calmness and control.

"Yes, Sergeant," she spoke slowly, with care, "I did send you the letter, but I believe I asked you to wait until after the holidays to call."

"I know, but I couldn't wait to make initial contact. I hope I haven't interrupted anything. You're not married?" His obvious reference to David's voice betrayed concern.

Lynn grew more confident and relaxed. "No, I'm not married. That was my brother who answered the phone. David and I share this apartment."

"Oh, good. Or rather, I'm glad. I really want to meet you, Lynn. That was a wonderful thing you did at the station. I'm staying with my parents, and your town is only a few miles away. I was wondering if we could get together tonight.

"It's New Year's Eve, Sergeant..."

"Andy. I'm separated from active duty now."

"Andy. It's a bit short notice for New Year's Eve."

"Of course you have a date. I'd just hoped."

"I don't have a date," Lynn considered how to handle the nature of her situation, "but I do have plans for the evening. I had asked you to wait until after the New Year."

"Yes. Normally I follow instructions. I guess the rush of changes being back - I just returned from Vietnam - are proving a bit much. I didn't want you to drive off again."

"Wait a minute. How do you know where I live?" It finally registered that the soldier had apparently identified her town.

"From your phone number prefix. Should I not have done that?"

"It's alright. I just hadn't thought of it." Relieved that her caller's source of information was not more threatening, Lynn dismissed her concern. His reference to Vietnam, though, had struck a resonant note, albeit through David's experience. She held fire for a moment, thinking, then plunged on. "I did recognize at the station that you were on your way home from Vietnam. I recognized your patch. My brother had been in that same division. That's kind of what led me to overreact. It was probably unwise."

Andy began to speak, but Lynn cut him off.

"I'm afraid it's just not possible to meet tonight." Lynn had quickly fashioned a plan she thought would provide some level of security. "Tomorrow is a holiday, but the Brookfield Zoo is always open. Do you know where the Brookfield Zoo is?"

"Roger that."

Lynn chuckled to herself upon hearing the standard army confirmation, but was careful to reveal no familiarity with it. "We could meet about three o'clock, say, in the Primate House. It's the first building on the left after entering the south gate.

"That will be great. I'll be there. But can we talk for a bit now?"

"I'm sorry, Andy. I have to go. I will see you tomorrow. Have a good New Year's Eve."

Lynn hung up the phone and walked to the patio door where she watched the final rays of the sun withdraw from the apartment complex' central square. As the last direct light descended below the top of the building to the west, she checked the clock, and her pensive study relaxed to a gentle smile.

"The sun is coming back," she said to herself, then turned from the winter scene outside to begin preparing for the night ahead.

4.

The returning sun she had tracked the previous evening had traveled from its disappearance in the west to beginning its appearance in the east when Lynn drove into the parking lot in front of her home, parked, and, holding up the hem of her long evening gown, ran across the snowy pavement to her building. She thought it well that she encountered no one enroute to her apartment, as the long night that had stretched into morning left her a bit disheveled and, she feared, perhaps showing a bit of beard growth.

Safely inside, she went immediately to the bedroom, dropped her coat on the floor, kicked off her shoes, pulled off her long gloves, unzipped her dress, all of which joined her coat on the floor. Conscious of her afternoon tryst, she set her alarm for noon and quickly fell asleep.

At twelve o'clock, awakened, she reluctantly forced herself to sit up and connect with the new year. Making no effort to put away the previous evening's clothing, she stumbled down the hallway, discarding underwear along the way, and stepped naked into the shower.

Two and a half hours later, refreshed and wearing a beneath her short winter coat a turtle neck sweater and, though she regretted the preclusion of a dress, blue jeans and flat heeled winter boots that would afford the freedom to run or defend herself should either be necessary, Lynn drove up to the ticket kiosk at the Brookfield Zoo's south parking lot, paid her admission, and then, in the virtually deserted lot, chose a space near the gate to the zoo grounds. She tightened the belt of her coat against the cold as she walked past the open iron gates and through the arched passage of the entrance building and once inside the zoo, surveying the expanse of winter-dormant promenade stretching north across the entire park, was pleased to see that, as she had expected, there were no other visitors to be seen.

She continued on, bearing left past the closed gift shop toward the first large building. Cages lining the structure's exterior were empty, barren, and filled with drifts of snow. She walked hurriedly to the doorway above which bas-relief monkeys flank the carved designation "Primates."

The rush of moist tropical heat that engulfed her when she stepped inside was startling, but welcome, and she paused just inside the entrance to acclimatize. She ignored the large cages that line the interior walls of the Primate House, focusing instead on the vast, barred enclosure reaching to the lofty ceiling and dominating the center of the huge, single room.

There, leaning against the observers' rail, but intently watching the doorway rather than the graceful gibbons swinging among the artificial trees of the cage was a solitary figure. As Lynn shook off the chill of the outside, the man left the rail and walked quickly toward her. He hesitantly held out his hand, addressing her as he approached.

"Lynn," he said, betraying intense relief, "you came."

"Hello, Andy," Lynn offered a gloved hand in response. "Happy New Year." Cautious and a bit anxious, she spoke softly and slowly, striving for femininity without comic exaggeration. Looking beyond her new acquaintance to the large central cage, she extracted, with a bit of effort, her hand from his.

"It's wonderfully warm in here," she observed, walking toward the exhibit.

Andy fell in beside her, his gaze fixed on her.

"Did you have a good New Year's Eve?" he asked.

Lynn nodded affirmation and continued her progress until she reached the waist high railing on which she placed both of her hands as she observed the acrobatic gibbons.

"I feel a bit awkward," Andy confessed, stepping beside her to the railing, but keeping his focus on her face.

Lynn looked up at the tall former soldier beside her. "Why is that?" she asked.

"This whole ad in the paper thing. I've never done anything like that, but I knew no other way to find you. I didn't really have much hope. I'm glad I did it, though. This is like a dream come true."

Hoping to use her voice as little as possible to minimize the risk of mistake, Lynn simply offered a look of amused skepticism.

"Really," Andy defended his perceived exaggeration, "I'm serious. When I first saw you walking toward me at the station, it was as though I was seeing someone I'd known, but lost; someone I'd dreamed of for a very long time."

Lynn turned to face Andy, but took a step back.

"Andy," she admonished, "you're just back from Vietnam. I know - I watched my brother try to adjust. It was hard. Everything seems so unreal." Realizing the length of her speech, she stopped and turned back to face the cage.

Andy said nothing for a moment, then reached inside his coat pocket and extracted a thick, carefully folded sheet of paper. Slowly, almost reverently, he flattened it out. "I wanted you to see this," he said, holding it out.

Lynn took the page, apparently torn from an art pad, and studied the artwork it bore: a quite masterfully rendered pencil drawing of a rice paddy and beyond that several thatched roof homes of a small Vietnamese village. Though a fact she clearly could not reveal, Lynn appreciated the accuracy of the depiction. Most startling, though, drawn large in the near foreground, was the upper torso of an occidental girl. Amazingly, she bore an uncanny resemblance to Lynn. Her hairstyle was identical, and her face eerily similar. At the bottom right corner of the drawing were the initials "A. J." and the date, written in army form, 22 Jun 71.

"You drew this?" she asked.

"Affirmative."

"It's really good. You're an artist?"

"I hope to be, but that's not the point. Don't you see the resemblance?"

Lynn looked again at the drawing, further confirming the undeniable fact that she could well have modeled the girl depicted.

"And yet," Andy continued, "I drew that - and others - from imagination long before I'd ever seen you. You understand how seeing you in real life at the station seemed a prayer answered."

"It's a wonderful drawing, Andy, but obviously, though similar, it's not me." Lynn held out the drawing, but Andy declined it.

"I want you to have it," he said.

"O. K. Thank you." Lynn folded the paper and put it into her purse, but as she did so she also sought to establish some limit to the length of the meeting and her level of risk. "I don't have much time," she said, walking toward the exit door. "I'm meeting my brother for dinner tonight and should get going soon, but I thought that if we hurried, we could watch the big cats get fed. That's something to see. You could tell me more about yourself while we walk over to the lion house."

Andy agreed, as he likely would have done to any suggestion Lynn were to make, and the two stepped out of the tropical warmth into the harshness of Chicago's winter. They walked swiftly north, circling the Teddy Roosevelt fountain, frozen and dormant at the juncture of the zoo's major eat-west and north-south promenades. As they walked, Lynn only half listened to Andy's words, allowing much of her consciousness to absorb the physical experience, the fullness her breasts imparted to her coat and the thrill of walking beside a man who believed her to be a woman and who was so clearly intent on pleasing her with his explanation of himself.

Andy spoke enthusiastically. He made no direct mention of his time in Vietnam, something Lynn understood. Instead, he regaled her with his dreams, his love for art, and the future upon which he, now separated from the army, was embarking, a future that involved beginning classes at the Art Institute of Chicago. His willingness to monopolize the conversation perfectly accommodated Lynn, whose greatest anxiety involved having to speak.

They were the only figures moving across the snow-swept, uninviting parkways, and that, too, suited Lynn. Near the zoo's north entrance she guided Andy to their right and into the warm and distinctively pungent Large Feline House. As they passed through the entrance foyer, in response to the heat, Lynn untied the belt of her coat and undid its buttons.

There were several other visitors, gathered as were Andy and Lynn, her temporal estimate having proved accurate, for feeding time. The panthers, lions, leopards, and tigers were pacing, bellowing, roaring, and coughing in anticipation as a keeper moved along the row of cages wheeling a cart laden with raw meat. Andy suspended personal discussion while he and Lynn shadowed the keeper's progress and watched the graceful and powerful cats voraciously devour the huge amounts of meat tossed with a dull thud into each successive cage.

When the last animal had been served, Lynn decided she had pressed her luck sufficiently. "I have to go, Andy," she said, buttoning up against the imminent cold. "We can talk some more on the way back."

"It seems to be just me talking," her companion noted, but Lynn merely smiled and he again fell in step beside her.

They left the lion house through doors at the end of the building opposite that through which they had entered, and their path took them past the zoo's long, terraced restaurant, abandoned for the season, and along the wide, sloping walk beside the outdoor bear pits. As the animals were inside for the winter, the displays were unoccupied, and the pathway similarly devoid of other human visitors. In spite of the cold, Andy and Lynn walked rather desultorily, pausing occasionally to read the placards describing what they would have seen had it been a warmer season. After they passed the uninhabited Asian Black Bear home, though, they encountered another couple huddled against the cold and watching a pair of extremely active Polar Bears, the lone species remaining outdoors.

Stopping a bit apart from the other couple, Andy and Lynn also watched with some amusement the antics of the two arctic animals. Calmly, almost slyly, Andy reached out and grasped Lynn's hand. Startled, Lynn reflexively pulled her hand back, but then reconsidered, welcoming the heightened physical and emotional experience, and let her hand remain in Andy's.

Tacitly accepting this new level of relationship, the two walked on, soon reaching the end of the row of bear pits and turning left on the central promenade, making their way toward the exit. One final building intervened between them and the gatehouse, and as they passed the walkway leading to it, Lynn stopped and pulled Andy back.

"It's the Small Mammal House." She pointed to their left. "Let's go in, just for a minute. I want to see if the aardvark has moved. He never does. I think he's stuffed."

She led Andy toward the large, columned building and up the concrete steps to a set of double doors with darkened glass. Inside, the two visitors had to pass around a wall that further restricts the entrance of light, a barrier necessitated by the fact that most of the animals of the Small Mammal House are nocturnal.

Lynn walked quickly through the eerily green darkness around a large, central glass case home to hundreds of flitting, frenetic, or just upside down hanging bats. She led Andy down a side wing and stopped in front of a large window beside a sign identifying the display's inhabitant to be an aardvark.

While she waited for her eyes to fully adjust to the subdued light, Lynn once more accommodated herself to the warmth by unbuttoning her coat.

"He's always asleep," she explained, referring to their quarry. "I've been coming here since I was a young child, and I've never seen him move." She peered intently into an almost impenetrably dark area of the habitat. "I think he's that darker mass in the corner. See?"

The two aardvark hunters concentrated in silence, leaning close to the glass, staring into the darkened habitat, seeking to spot the elusive anteater. As moments passed, Andy's interest proved less engaged than was his companion's. He glanced about the wing they occupied and discovered it to be as deserted, other than for themselves, as much of the zoo had proven to be. He looked down at Lynn and took her hand again, applying a gentle pressure that Lynn returned.

"I see him," she said with an excitement that nearly betrayed a potentially disastrous, unfeminine voice.

She pointed into the exhibit and turned to see if Andy were following her lead. He wasn't. She discovered herself to be the full focus of his attention and, surprised, could offer only an awkward and ineffective, "See?"

Andy released her hand and thrust both of his inside her coat, around her waist, drawing her close. Instinctively, defensively, Lynn pulled her elbows in and raised her hands to Andy's shoulders, providing some protection where their bodies were about to touch. She yielded without struggle, though, to his kiss.

Feeling its passion, she briefly contemplated its hazards, but surrendered intellect to sensuality. She responded with warmth, thrilling to the sexuality of the embrace and kiss, but as her own passion increased, she felt its inevitable effect stir between her legs, and, fearing imminent discovery, pushed herself away. Clearly flustered, disturbed, she struggled to regain control, drawing her coat close about her.

"I'm sorry, Andy," she whispered.

"I guess I presumed too much," he said a bit forlornly, taking a step to follow Lynn's retreat.

"No. That's not it," Lynn answered, backing farther off. "It's just that... sudden... I really must go."

Buttoning her coat, she walked around the puzzled ex-soldier and made her way to the exit. Outside in the frigid and bright air, she regained composure and waited for Andy to catch up.

He approached her tentatively, uncertain. "Are you offended?" he asked.

Lynn smiled reassuringly. "No, certainly not. I'm just going to be late. Walk me to my car." She took his hand again and they walked beneath the arch of the gatehouse into the parking lot.

"Can I see you again?" Andy asked as Lynn opened her car door.

"Yes, of course."

"Tomorrow?" he pressed. "It's Friday. You don't have a date, do you?"

"No, but I do have something going on, and it can't be changed. Call me Saturday about 6 P. M., and we can arrange something. And," she offered Andy a gentle touch to soften her demand, "please observe the schedule this time." She placed one foot into her car, then stepped back out and repeated the scene from the train station, placing a hand on his cheek and kissing him, and as he had been at the station, Andy was forced to simply watch as Lynn left in a departing vehicle.

5.

Again seeking his wisened counsel, Lynn reached out to Barry, driving early the next evening to "Charlie's," arriving well before a weekend crowd would command his attention. Her plan was successful; there were only two other patrons in the bar when she arrived, and when Barry brought her drink, she was able to detain him.

"I could really use some advice." She introduced her dilemma. "You've been around girls like me a long time..,"

"Don't start on age, hon," Barry interrupted. "I can always find some glasses to wash."

"That's not what I meant. You just have more ...never mind. Here's my problem. You remember you advised me to drop this soldier involvement?"

"Can I assume you haven't?"

"Yes, I guess you can. Hear me out, Barry, please." Lynn had to restrain the bartender's disgusted turn to move away. "I sent him my phone number; he called, and we met. I had him meet me at the Brookfield Zoo yesterday. That seemed a safe place. We spent about an hour together."

"You didn't tell him the truth? He didn't suspect?"

"No, and apparently not. It seems I'm the incarnation of a vision he had in Vietnam. He showed me a picture he'd drawn, and the girl in it looks uncannily like me. He's an artist."

"He's a nut and he's going to beat the crap out of you. He's just a few hours from a war zone."

Seeking to reassure Barry, Lynn placed a hand on his arm and leaned forward. "He's not like that. I can understand where he's been and what it's like coming home. I can…"

"But you didn't tell him how you can understand."

"That's true. I suggested that I knew some things because of my brother."

"Brother David, no doubt." Barry's frustration was clearly growing.

"Yes, actually, but listen. Lose the insane Vietnam veteran stereotype. Andy's not like that. He's an artist. He'll be going to the Art Institute this semester. He's a sensitive person."

Barry collected his thoughts, attempting to assimilate the story Lynn was relating. "At least," he seized upon some sort of consolation, "you didn't encourage physical contact."

Lynn sat back. "Well,…"

"Oh, please."

"It's not really something I should discuss, but we held hands and then in the Small Mammal House he kissed me."

"Right in the Small Mammal House."

"Spare me the attempt at humor. It was wonderful. I'd never been kissed by someone who thought I was a real woman."

Apparently seeking to temper his response, Barry waited, then tried once more to urge caution. "Lynn," he carefully began, "this soldier's been overseas for an entire year. He's going to want more than a kiss, and when he goes after it, you're going to get hurt. As you so delicately suggest, I've been around the girls at 'Charlie's' for a long time and I've never known one who could pull off fooling an unwitting straight guy for long."

"I know I can't mislead him forever - I'm not delusional - but he's had this dream, and Lynn is apparently it. I believe he can deal with the truth."

"You're going to see him again?"

Lynn nodded. "Tomorrow night."

"How does Randy fit into all this?"

"There's no conflict. From the start Randy's been all about sex, and it's worked for us. I guess my idea of what constitutes sensuality has altered a bit."

"Do you think you and this soldier are going to fall in love?" Barry interjected with some antagonism.

"No," Lynn seemed clear, "love is not the issue. The purpose of male involvement is just to enable being female. I guess it's just that with this soldier, there is more than merely physical sex. It's something more. There could be romance involved; something real women experience. That's what I'm seeking: authentic female experience."

Barry was unconvinced. "You claim to want advice, but you're obviously determined to ignore my best counsel, so at least listen to this. Don't be alone with him. Don't go to his place, or..."

"He's living with his parents."

"Or have him up to yours. You think he'll accept the truth, so give it to him over the phone. If he seems to accept it, then see him again in a safe place with other people around. You say he thinks he's found some sort of dream. You're feeding it, building it up. Destroying that could be worse than if he were just looking for a quick lay."

Barry noticed one of the other customers on the other side of the bar waiting for him and beginning to lose patience. "Excuse me," he said, little disguising the fact that he'd had enough of Lynn's intransigence and welcomed the excuse to end the discussion. "Be safe."

The rest of the night and throughout the next day Lynn thought of little other than the feminine sensuality she had experienced with Andy and the warnings presented by Barry. She knew the latter to be wise, but the former was compelling. She formed dozens of plans, each in conflict with its predecessor, but by the time for Andy's call, she had found what she felt to be a compromise.

Andy followed instructions with the precision of a soldier, and at precisely 6 P. M. her phone rang.

"You're prompt, soldier," she strove for lightheartedness.

"You said six," Andy answered. "I've been watching the time. I'd like to take you to dinner. Give me your address, and I can be over to pick you up in a few minutes. I'm anxious to see you again."

"That's sweet, Andy. I'm looking forward to being with you again, also. Dinner would be wonderful, but I was hoping I could convince you to meet me at a place I know, a nightclub in one of the northern suburbs. It's a great place, and being with me there would help you learn more about me."

"I've known all about you for months, Lynn. Why can't I pick you up at home? You said you're not married. Is your brother a problem?"

"Certainly not. Not exactly. It's just that I have an errand to do for him that's taking me up to the north side anyway, and we could just meet at this place, 'Charlie's.' I'll give you directions."

Andy protested a bit more, but, though skeptical, eventually capitulated and agreed to be at "Charlie's" at nine o'clock.

Intending to grease the skids for Andy's introduction to "Charlie's" and also to herself, Lynn arrived at the tavern at eight o'clock, assessed the crowd, and selected, for hosting her unsuspecting guest, a table tucked far in the back end of the room.

"Back again?" Barry questioned the obvious when Lynn stepped up to the bar to order a drink. "I thought you would have a date with Audie Murphy tonight."

"It's Andy, and I do. I took your advice and arranged for him to meet me here. It should be easy to explain to him here."

Barry was less than pleased. "You're having him come here completely unaware of what he's walking into? That's crazy. He may go off and do some damage or harm. No one here wants the police brought in. Call him and stop him."

"I can't. I don't know his number. Besides, he's probably already on his way. I tell you, Barry, there won't be a problem. I promise."

"If there is, and police get involved, you'll be the object of a lot of really intense anger. You won't ever be able to come here again."

Undaunted, Lynn proceeded. "Could you put a 'reserved' or 'out of order' sign, or something on that last table in the back? That's where I'm going to take him to talk. It's out of the way."

Resigned, Barry agreed to Lynn's plan. "I'll turn the chairs over on the table for now. And you can have it when you want, but I'm going to let the bouncer in on this and make sure he watches when Sergeant York gets here. This is not, though, a very good idea. Hormones must be deranging your thinking. I'm going to hold you responsible if anything goes wrong. You're presuming a lot on our friendship, Lynn."

"I know, but it means a lot to me, Barry. It will be all right. You'll see."

In order to intercept Andy as soon as possible when he entered, Lynn took possession of a stool just around the bar's curve, one affording a clear field of vision of the entrance and, with the tavern only sparsely populated, an unfettered pathway to it. As Andy's scheduled arrival time approached, Lynn focused more intently on the doorway, though she periodically assessed the activity in the bar and convinced herself that "Charlie's'" - after all, a very low profile, neighborhood sort of establishment - patrons generally maintained calm, subdued behavior, sufficiently non-flamboyant, she reasoned, to preclude sudden shock for the uninitiated. She reasoned that she could probably steer Andy to the back table before he discovered the irregularities of the bar's clientele.

Her hopes were justified when Andy did walk in: he searched so intently for his date that he took little notice of anyone not her. Lynn called Barry over.

"He made formation." In response to the barkeep's puzzled look, she explained, indicating Andy as he stood, adjusting his eyes to the dim room. "He's on time. A good soldier always makes formation."

"So that's the ambush victim. He is good looking. Definitely a Wally

Cleaver. You may be right about trouble being unlikely, but I'll advise security."

Lynn jumped up from her stool just as Andy spotted her and they quickly came together in a somewhat awkward embrace.

"This place is hard to find. It's nearly unmarked." Andy was smiling broadly at the woman he came to see. "You weren't kidding about the sign, I had to hunt to spot it."

Becoming accustomed to the lighting, Andy began to look around, but Lynn reached up for his cheek, redirected his attention to herself, and began to lead him toward the back of the tavern.

"I have a table waiting for us, Andy."

She moved quickly, dragging Andy along, hoping to minimize his inspection of "Charlie's'" people. When they reached the reserved table, Andy helped her set the chairs on the floor and, without really taking his eyes from her, removed his coat and held one of the chairs out for her.

They sat, and Lynn placed her purse on the table and took both of Andy's hands in hers, fervently securing his attention.

"I'm so glad you were willing to come, Andy. There is so much I want to tell you. Barry the Bartender will bring us some drinks. I ordered a beer for you. Is that right?"

"Perfect," Andy assented, "just like you. I've tried to explain to my parents about you, but they can't seem to appreciate how amazing it is that I've found you."

"Well, Andy," Lynn began to introduce her revelation, "amazing might not be the half of it. Remember how I told you my brother had been in your unit, had been to Vietnam..."

"Wait." Andy's attention had slipped to some people on the dance floor. He squinted his eyes in puzzlement and withdrew his attention from Lynn, who desperately held on to his hands. "Something's funny over there," he began to watch more intently. "There are two guys dancing together."

Unfortunately for Lynn, at just that moment one of the taller and less convincing girls walked with undisguised masculine stride across the dance floor heading for the restroom.

"That's a strange woman." Andy began to grasp his situation. "That's a guy. What is this? Some sort of a queer bar?" He turned abruptly to Lynn and pulled his hands away. "Why did you bring me here?"

"I wanted you to understand, Andy. I'm not ...I 'm not exactly a genetic woman."

Andy's expression grew intense, horrified. He pushed his chair back from the table.

"You're a queer!" he nearly shouted. "You tricked me. You said you understood how I felt, what it is like coming back from Vietnam, because of your brother. You..."

Lynn tried to regain control as Andy stammered in confusion.

"I do understand, Andy. It's just that it wasn't my brother who was in Vietnam, it was me. I've been where you've been. Andy, I'm not really homosexual. I'm not trying to be a man with men. I'm becoming a woman. Look." She dug into her purse, pulled out the drawing Andy had given her, and unfolded it on the table. "This drawing is real. Its dream is still real. I can be that girl."

Andy grabbed the drawing, crumpled it into a ball, and tossed it onto the floor. "No you can't." He lashed out. "You can't be any girl. This just makes everything disgusting."

Turning furiously away, Andy crashed into Barry who was delivering the two drinks.

"Get out of my way," Andy growled, giving Barry a shove. Incensed, he roughly pushed his way across the dance floor, around the bar, and out the door.

"That went well." Barry, whose experienced expertise had saved the beer and Vodka and 7-Up from disaster, sat down with Lynn and handed her the mixed drink.

"I'll take them both," she said, "and there's no need to be sarcastic. This isn't funny."

"Actually, I was sincere," Barry said. "No violence. No need for security or the police. You're still whole, and the place is unscathed."

"Whole. Yes." Lynn took a drink and reached to the floor to retrieve the drawing. "You were right, Barry, and I was wrong. He called this disgusting. David's heard that from Randy. I'm tired of some people being disgusted when thinking of me as David, and others just as disgusted to think of me as Lynn." She flattened out the drawing, studied it for a moment, then looked at the bartender. "I don't want to be disgusting. I don't want to dress up in women's clothes. I want to simply dress in my clothes. I don't want to have to think about being female. I..." she stopped and recrumpled the drawing.

"Hon," Barry indicated the crowd of patrons, "I can't stay. Are you going to be all right? Come over to the bar and stay close."

"I'll be fine, Barry. I just need to think this through. It seems that you were right; Randy's right. I guess Jeannie is right. Everyone but me is right. Something needs to change."

CHAPTER SIX

A Season in New York

1.

Lynn lay on her back watching the stars arrayed above her drift slowly across an unusually clear, late July sky. Raising her head from the mattress she had hauled from her apartment to the roof of the building and placed on cinder blocks and plywood, she could see the lights of barges and ships navigating the East River, and beyond the river, the brilliant towers of Manhattan looming brightly, overpowering stars that would have been visible above a natural horizon. In contrast to the frenetic human hustle just across the water, Lynn's Vernon Boulevard, Long Island City, Queens, neighborhood was as quiet as the vast heavens overhead. It had always amazed Lynn that many Long Island City residents rarely crossed the river to Manhattan.

During weekday commuting hours, the southernmost blocks of Vernon Boulevard are an active, bustling neighborhood, but nightlife is the province of other, more lustrous areas of New York City. Truncated by the Long Island Expressway at its descent into the mid-town tunnel to Manhattan, the boulevard's dead end comprises a tiny, but pleasant park, the most important element of which is the final subway station in

Queens, one stop from Grand Central Station. The subway entrance draws thousands of commuters each weekday, but the significant life, energy, and commerce of the neighborhood remain those of a traditional, insular enclave of mostly Italian heritage inhabitants.

With the single exception of "Bellomini's Bar," an institution that never closes, simply drawing its blinds to ignore city ordinances and to admit - with the tacit disinterest of local law enforcement - at any hour those who are known, the area shuts down at night as tightly as any small Midwestern town.

It was surprising, then, when the sound of an approaching automobile disturbed the evening's silence. Even more surprisingly, the auto stopped somewhere near Lynn's building. She rolled over on the mattress and cautiously, much like a soldier conducting an ambush, peered over the roof's low rampart. Across the street "Bellomini's," hosting the anointed, cast a warm glow of subdued light through the drawn blinds, and to both the left and right, the street, as she expected it would be, was deserted.

Searching for the source of the sound that had interrupted her peace, Lynn stretched a bit farther over the ledge and discovered, three stories below and just in front of her doorway, a car parked at the curb. While she watched, two men stepped out of the vehicle and quietly pushed its doors shut.

Though from Lynn's perspective the men were just tops of heads and moving arms and legs, she thought she recognized one to be the tenant of an apartment above the tobacco store across the street from her building. The other was clearly bald. Confirming her surmise about the former, the two men crossed the street to the doorway leading to the apartment above the tobacconist's shop.

The bald man, waiting for his companion to unlock the door, turned to the street and looked up at the sky. Instinctively, Lynn lowered her profile, just barely peering over the edge. She could see that though the unknown man had no hair on his head, he boasted a thick and full mustache. When the two men had disappeared into the building, Lynn gazed idly for a few moments at the once more vacant scene below, then rolled back over to resume watching the stars. Her mood, however, had been spoiled, and she sat up, grabbed her T-shirt from beside the mattress and pulled it on, tugging it a bit to watch it form over her small, almost child-like breasts that more than six months of hormone therapy had developed. She cupped a hand over each breast, savoring the sensation of each one's shape.

Content, she rose, pulled a protective plastic cover over the mattress, and walked across the roof to the rear of the building. Stepping over the edge, she placed a foot on a steel ladder affixed to the wall and climbed down one flight to another roof. Beside the ladder at its base was an open window through which Lynn climbed into her home.

Carved from a former factory floor, the apartment was really one large room. An added bathroom occupied most of one side of the apartment, leaving a narrow alcove that had been outfitted as a kitchen. A larger second alcove, partially closed off by a tall Japanese screen and containing a double bed, dresser and an armoire, served as a bedroom.

Lynn placed an expandable screen into the open window, then edged her way around her couch and a brick pillar that testified to the apartment's former incarnation and entered the bathroom, emerging some minutes later wearing a long, lacy nightgown. A few steps brought her to the bedroom alcove where, after a half hour spent reading, she fell asleep.

Just at dawn the next morning, beating her alarm clock, as she usually did, she sprang from bed fully awake. She opened the armoire door and placed her nightgown on a hook, pausing, naked, to look down at her breasts, just touching them gently with the fingers of each hand. The ring of her alarm, however, caught up, urging her to begin preparations for her ritual morning run.

As a concession to her most significant remaining element of maleness, she carefully arranged a tight pair of running shorts and covered them with some baggy sweat pants, pulled on a sports bra, tied her long hair into a ponytail, and began the five minutes of stretching that preceded a bound out the door and a run down two flights of stairs and through the building's small lobby to the street.

She drew the pleasant morning air deeply into her lungs and performed a few final stretches. Though the sidewalks were not particularly crowded, increasing numbers of people were moving south along Vernon Boulevard, the early trickles of a human stream that would grow to a torrent flowing from the north to be joined by others from the east and west, all headed for the tiny park and its entrance to the subway that each weekday bore massive numbers of workers beneath the river to Manhattan.

Lynn began her run, threading her way through the early morning commuters, many of whom were entering or leaving "Nick's Restaurant," having set out early enough to enjoy breakfast at the diner on the western side of the park. She ran to the corner south of her building and turned right onto a still deserted street of modest bungalow homes scattered among nondescript warehouses and wholesale businesses, then crossed the empty parking lot of a tennis club housed beneath a large fabric dome.

Running out of street, she turned north at the edge of the river and ran steadily on along cracking concrete that had served an apparently once vibrant riverfront. Decayed, abandoned, weathered, and rotted wharves and isolated, moss covered poles rising in defiant survival above lapping waves outlined the forms of long collapsed piers. Ahead of Lynn throughout this leg of her run loomed the soaring arch of the 59th Street Bridge connecting the Boroughs of Queens and Manhattan.

Though raucous seabirds and loudly intrusive boat traffic occasionally caught her attention, her focus as she ran north was on the bridge, on its gracious, triumphant engineering that dominated the view before her. With a bit of regret she at last reached it and ran east beneath its gargantuan pillars for several blocks until she reconnected with Vernon Boulevard and turned south toward home.

None of the charm of the riverfront favored the return portion of her run. She negotiated traffic, pedestrians, and in one particularly tricky block, the tangle of nighttime cab drivers returning their hacks to their garage and the waiting day crew.

Approaching within a few blocks of the boulevard's end, she discerned unusual activity, apparently near her home. Red and blue lights were flashing, and there seemed to be a crowd gathered.

Running closer, she discovered that police cars and an ambulance had closed off the final block of the boulevard and that people forming the crowd, rather than moving toward the subway, were milling about the building across the street from her own. Using the last block as a cooldown, Lynn slowed to a walk and approached the crowd from its rear, seeking to discover the nature of the commotion.

"What's going on?" she asked a particularly tall man straining to look over the top of the mass of onlookers.

"Well." He hesitated briefly to rather quizzically study his questioner, then, apparently satisfied, continued. "I think someone has died in there." He indicated the building with the tobacco store on its first floor. "I heard there was a murder."

Unable to see over the heads of those between herself and the putative crime scene and tired and sweaty from her run, Lynn decided to inquire no further and walked over to the entrance to her building, engaged in a few finishing stretches, and went inside.

2.

Quickly shedding her running gear, Lynn passed from the apartment door to the bathroom where she took a shower, dried her hair, and applied makeup. She gathered the scattered articles of running clothing as she walked to the bedroom alcove, dropped them into a clothes hamper, and selected the morning's outfit from the armoire.

While attaching the second nylon stocking to her garter belt, she noticed the time displayed on her alarm clock and, surprised by the lateness of the hour, hurried the normally protracted pleasure of dressing.

She hooked a brassiere behind her back, and though her breasts still failed of actually needing one, she took great pride in no longer adding breast forms. She yanked her dress down over her head, stepped into a pair of high-heeled shoes, grabbed her purse from the dresser, rushed into the living area, and from a desk in one of the corners of the room selected several papers and notebooks, which she stuffed into an attaché case. She walked quickly to the door and pushed it open. Standing on the landing outside were two men in conservative business suits, one about to knock, and both as startled by Lynn's sudden appearance as was she by their unexpected presence.

"Oops," she stammered, "I didn't know anyone was here." Regaining sufficient composure to address them, though not without sufficient caution to step back and pull the door partially shut, she asked, "Can I help you?"

The two men stood one behind the other and both presented serious, rather somber aspects. The one who had raised his hand, about to knock, was sturdy, stocky, possessed of a rather puffy, bent nose - the nose of someone who had perhaps spent some time in a boxing ring - and conspicuously large ears, their size accentuated by a severely short haircut. He was somewhat younger and considerably taller than his partner, who himself was far from short, and, opening his suit coat, he presented a police badge and identification.

"I'm sorry we startled you, Ma'am," he said with a gravelly, yet gently pleasant voice. "I'm Detective Anderson, and this," he indicated the scowling man behind him, "is Detective Matthews. There has been some trouble across the street, and we're just checking through the neighborhood to ask if people heard or saw anything unusual last night. Probably sometime after midnight."

Lynn's attention during the detective's speech was held by his silent, somewhat menacing companion. Only vaguely listening to the former's words, she stared into the latter's eyes, which were similarly locked on her own. Detective Matthews also apparently ignored his partner.

"The name on the mailbox in the lobby says, 'D. Stewart,'" he brusquely interrupted. "Is that you?"

"I'm sorry, what?" Lynn was rattled by the policeman's intensity.

"Do you reside here? Are you D. Stewart?"

Flustered, Lynn hesitated. "Yes, I live here," she finally got out. "I am D. Stewart."

Detective Anderson opened a small notebook, but before he could begin questioning Lynn, the other officer nudged him aside and directly confronted her.

"It's Mister D. Stewart, is it not?" He shot the "Mister" out as an accusation. "Is that for Dennis, or Denton, or what?" He took a step closer.

Lynn capitulated. "It's David."

As triumphant as Detective Anderson was dumbfounded, Matthews took over the inquiry.

"May we come in, Mr. Stewart?" Again he emphasized the masculine title.

Lynn stepped back and directed the two policemen to the living area. They took the offered seats on the couch, and Lynn sat, awkwardly self-conscious, on the chair turned from her desk. The younger detective remained silent, observing his partner continue the questioning.

"So, Mr. Stewart," Detective Matthews nearly growled, "we have what appears to be a homicide in your neighborhood. One..." he looked to Anderson, who failed to follow the lead. "What's the victim's name, Anderson?"

"Name. Oh, yes," Anderson pulled himself back to duty. "Jason Victor."

Matthews turned to Lynn. "Yes, Jason Victor. He lived on the second floor above the tobacconist. Did you know him, Sir?"

Still apparently unable to reconcile his partner's, "Sir," with the person to whom it was addressed, the younger detective glanced quickly back and forth between the other officer and Lynn.

"No," Lynn responded. "I'd seen him a few times on the street. I didn't know his name and I've never spoken with him."

"Well, we believe he may have been murdered," Matthews said.

"Really? That's... astounding." Lynn fidgeted, growing increasingly uncomfortable clutched in Matthew's unflinching stare.

"It appears he was gay, Mr. Stewart."

"Ah." Lynn grasped the detective's implication. "I see." The unsubtle suggestion served to inspire some defensive spark. "Well, I didn't know him, Detective, and actually, as I suspect you know, most gay men have little interest in someone such as myself."

Matthew's smug affirmation carried the weight of accusation. "Perhaps that was a problem." Preventing an attempted response from Lynn, Matthews drove on. "Were you home last night, Sir?"

"Yes."

"Alone?"

"Yes."

Removing, for the first time, his focus from Lynn's face, Matthews looked about the apartment. "Your window gives out to the west, not to the street side. Did you by any chance go out, perhaps to "Bellomini's?" His smirk revealed how unlikely he believed it to be that Lynn would patronize the local bar.

"No, but I did see the victim ... the deceased last night."

Matthews, suddenly sincerely interested in what Lynn had to say, inadvertently softened his gaze. "And when and how was this?" He dropped the "Sir" and "Mr. Stewart."

"I had worked most of the evening. It was warm, so when I quit, I went up on the roof to watch the stars for a while before going to sleep. It's relaxing. There's a ladder outside my window," she indicated the window behind the detectives, "and I've put a mattress up there for comfort."

"A mattress. You say you were alone."

Lynn shot Matthews her own angered gaze. "Yes, alone. Anyway, Vernon Boulevard is a pretty quiet street in the night, and I heard a car pull up and stop, so I looked over the edge of the roof."

"Go on."

"A car had parked in front of my building, and two men got out. One was the guy who lived across the street, and they crossed over to his place."

"You could recognize them?"

"I don't know who the other man is, but I recognized ... what's his name."

"Victor Jason," the younger detective was this time prompt with his information.

"Yes," Lynn acknowledged the help. "He was right below me. Besides, they went in his door."

"What time was this?" Matthews glanced at his partner to confirm that notes were being taken.

"I'm not certain. Not long before 2 A. M., I guess, because that's what my clock said when I went to bed. I didn't stay on the roof long after they had arrived."

"Who was driving?"

"The other man."

"Can you identify the car?"

"Not precisely. I'm not much of a car person, and at night the street-lights tend to wash out colors. It was large, possibly dark blue. If I had to, I'd guess it was a Buick. The driver, though, I can tell you, is bald and has a large, bushy mustache."

"And how do you know that, Mr. Stewart?" Matthews had recovered his hostility.

"As I said, they were right below me. The man wore no hat, and while he was waiting for Victor to open the door, he looked up at the sky. Bald, mustache."

Matthews waited a moment for his partner's note taking to catch up, then continued his rather overtly antagonistic inquiry. "You were just on your way out, Sir?"

"Yes, I have an appointment in Manhattan with my agent."

"I see. You're an actor, then?"

"No," Lynn indicated the cluttered, paper covered desk and

typewriter, "I'm a writer." She noticed Detective Anderson, apparently startled, abruptly look up from his notebook and stare at her. "At least," she qualified, "I'm trying to be."

For the first time since Matthews had assumed the lead role, Anderson questioned Lynn. "You're a writer? You make your living writing? You've been published?"

Matthews' dismissive gesture cut off the other detective's questioning. "Well, Mr. Stewart," he turned back to Lynn, "you may have been one of the last persons to have seen Mr. Victor alive, other than the killer, that is. I'm afraid we're going to have to ask you to miss your appointment and come around to the precinct house to file a statement and look at some pictures to see if you can spot your mustachioed bald man."

Lynn glanced at the clock in her sleeping area and gave a resigned shrug. "I would be late now, anyway. Just give me a moment to call my agent and change."

"You needn't change, Mr. Stewart," Matthews exhibited a disturbingly snide smile. "You're fine just as you are."

Having conceded her exposure, Lynn was nonetheless unwilling to be subjected to possible humiliation on a larger and more formal scale. She faced Matthews with some defiance. "Am I under arrest, Detective? Do I need a lawyer?"

"No, No, Mr. Stewart, you're not under arrest."

"Then I'm coming voluntarily?"

"And we greatly appreciate it."

"Then wait." Lynn started for her bedroom. "I'll change."

Matthews grudgingly acquiesced.

After a quick call to her agent, Lynn pulled from beneath her bed a suitcase containing emergency David clothes and carried it into the bathroom.

Fifteen minutes later David emerged, clean of makeup, his hair in a ponytail, wearing blue jeans and a somewhat battered U. S. Army fatigue shirt that hung sufficiently loosely to hide his rather small, developing breasts.

His appearance elicited a scowl from Detective Matthews. Pointing to the Combat Infantry Badge on David's shirt, he gave vent to his disgust.

"Are you trying to be funny?" he growled. "You have no business wearing that badge of honor. Take that off"

David took the offensive. "I have every business wearing it. Check the name, Detective." He pointed to the nametag. "'Stewart.' This is my shirt. I earned the CIB in Vietnam. I have every right to wear it, and I intend to. Shall we go?"

With a disgusted shrug the elder detective started toward the door, but as he reached for the knob, he turned back. "By the way, Mr. Stewart, just what sort of writing do you do? Do you have any examples we could see?"

"Yes," David was a bit surprised by the request, and his exasperation grew, "I do, however, it's not much." He walked back into the living room area and from a corner shelf acquired a small book of short stories. "Here's a copy. If you think you can profit from reading it, you may have it."

"I'd like to see it," Detective Anderson eagerly responded to the offer and took possession of the book.

David followed the two detectives out of the apartment and, having locked the door behind himself, down the stairs.

3.

Though she had virtually no contact with neighbors, her apartment having been chosen for the fact that it was the only private residence in her building, Lynn sensed, after a week had passed, that the murder had ceased to be a consuming topic in Long Island City. Chance remarks overheard at a store or on the subway platform suggested that Vernon Boulevard had dismissed the episode as a rather welcome removal of an undesirable element.

The weather had become stiflingly hot, and in the late afternoon, seven days since she had presented her information at the police station, she slouched at her desk paying more attention to the bright sunlight streaming over the tops of the Manhattan towers and in through her window than to the pages of blank paper awaiting her words.

The summer heat had penetrated her large room, reaching into even the shaded bed and kitchen alcoves. Dismissing all pretense of working, Lynn walked over to the window, removed the screen, and, sitting on the sill, ducked under the raised pane, turning her legs, bare beneath a short summer skirt, out onto the roof. She sat thus, eyes closed, appreciating the gentle river breeze that offered some respite from the sun's warmth. An unexpected knock on her door, however, pulled her attention inside.

She bent back under the windowpane and listened for a few moments, unable to imagine who would be outside her door, but when the visitor rapped again, she pulled her legs inside and went to the door. Peering through the peephole, she was startled and a bit dismayed to see Detective Anderson waiting on the landing.

"Detective?" Lynn's greeting when she had opened her door was really a question, an anxious request for explanation.

"Hello, Miss ...Mister Stewart," the policeman answered. "May I come in?"

Lynn stepped back to allow the detective entry.

"Where's your delightful cohort?" She checked the landing and stairway for Anderson's partner.

"Detective Matthews isn't with me. He suggested I stop by and tell you that we have our killer."

"I'm very glad to hear that — both parts," Lynn said sincerely as she directed the policeman to the couch and took a seat on the desk chair. "How did you catch him?"

Anderson, focused on the floor, clearly ill at ease, explained. "We didn't exactly catch him; he turned himself in. It seems we have an instance of an enraged lovers' quarrel, not an act of premeditated murder."

"Bald with a bushy mustache?"

"Bald with a bushy mustache." For the first time Anderson looked directly at Lynn and smiled. "You were correct, Mister Stewart. Your..."

Lynn interrupted, "You seem less hostile than your partner, Detective. Would you mind calling me 'Miss Stewart' or 'Lynn?' I'd greatly appreciate it."

Anderson's awkward uncertainty returned. "Anyway," he continued, sidestepping Lynn's request, "your description was accurate, and we thank you for your willingness to cooperate."

"I assume you are speaking for yourself and not for Detective Matthews. Do you think I will be called to testify?"

"I doubt it. The perpetrator is cooperating, and I imagine the District Attorney's office will obtain a plea bargain."

The two sat, then, in silence, the detective again focused on the floor in front of him.

Assuming the interview to be concluded, Lynn rose from her chair. "I appreciate your consideration in stopping by, Detective Anderson," she offered. "I imagine it's been a bit difficult for you." As the policeman remained seated, giving no indication of departing, she asked, "Is there something else, Detective?"

"Well, yes," Anderson reached into his coat pocket and extracted Lynn's book of short stories and held it out to her. "I want to return your book."

"Thank you. You've read it?"

"Yes, I have."

"And Detective Matthews?"

"He asked me to report on it."

"No doubt he was hoping for some gay sado-masochistic porn." Lynn took the proffered volume.

Again Anderson smiled. "Something like that. But don't misjudge him. He's a good cop, a great one, actually. I've learned a lot working with him. He's committed to the law and to making the city safe, particularly, as he sees it, for his family. But anyway, as I said, I've read your book, and it's left me a bit confused."

"Oh?" With the conversation taking a new direction, Lynn sat down.

"The stories are excellent. "Anderson seemed to have some difficulty expressing himself. "Well written." He stopped.

"And you can't understand how someone like me," with a sweeping gesture Lynn alluded to her appearance and dress, "could write with any authority about war."

Anderson nodded affirmatively. "You were there?"

"Vietnam? I told you and your partner I was. Surely you checked."

"We did. I find it a difficult fact."

"Wait here. I have something to show you." Lynn rose from the chair and entered the bedroom alcove, retrieving from under the bed the David suitcase. She plopped it on the bed, opened it, and, after a bit of digging, located a photo album. Back in the living area she sat down beside the policeman, who edged a bit away.

"You don't mind if I sit here?" she responded to her guest's movement. "I only want to show you some pictures."

Unmistakably nervous, Anderson nonetheless assented to Lynn's intention to sit beside him and paid attention as she opened the album, holding it between them. She slowly flipped through pages of photographs of grungy, unkempt soldiers huddled in sandbag bunkers, wading rivers, struggling through dense, obscuring jungle. At one page she stopped and pointed out a picture of a thin, blond soldier in half-laced boots, jungle fatigue pants, and a brown T-shirt, holding an M-16 rifle and with a bandolier of ammunition tied around his waist. The soldier posed, smiling, in front of a thatched roof Vietnamese dwelling and beside a diminutive Asian soldier wearing flip-flops and pajamas.

"That's me," Lynn indicated, "the taller one." She smiled at her attempt at humor, but receiving no reaction, continued. "I look a bit different, but that is me, and I retain all the memories of my life. I haven't dramatically altered my brain."

Anderson took the album onto his lap, and while he studied the pictures, Lynn reflected on the realization that she had experienced no trouble addressing the fact of David's coexistence with her own, something that had invariably proven an anathema for Randy.

"Is all this really part of your investigation?" she eventually asked, unable to devise any other ploy to advance the policeman's visit to some identifiable end.

The detective closed the album and handed it back to her. "Interesting," he noncommittally observed. "And no, this has nothing to do with the investigation. I wanted to return your book and to speak with you about writing. It's something I've always wanted to do. I have written some stories, but I've never submitted anything for publication. I've never even let anyone see them." He ignored Lynn's incredulous expression. "You're the first successful author I've ever met, and I thought perhaps you could give me some advice."

"I don't think that one book of short stories that is making me neither rich nor famous qualifies as success."

"But it does. You've done something I have always wanted to do. I wonder if you would be willing to look at something I've written?" he asked.

Lynn studied the large, awkward, ill-at-ease policeman, carefully considering his request. "I'm not at all qualified to be either a critic or a mentor," she advised. "I can't even make a living at this. I pay the bills by writing greeting cards and freelance assignments like industrial catalogs. Hardly anything that can be considered literature." As the detective neither spoke nor indicated intention to leave, she relented. "Is it crime fiction?" she asked.

"No," Anderson fixed Lynn with an eager look, "I'd like to think it's more... general than that. I don't really know what it is, I guess. I certainly don't know if it's any good."

"I'd be honored to read your work, Detective."

Anderson seemed greatly relieved, as though a worrisome task had been accomplished, and he rose and walked toward the door. "Perhaps I could drop something off," he suggested as he opened the door and stepped onto the landing.

"You know where to find me."

Lynn shut her door behind the departed policeman and leaned back against it, considering what had just happened. She pondered briefly without appreciable result, then, giving it up, returned to the desk, picked up a pencil, and with an energy that had earlier eluded her, began to fill previously blank pages.

4.

A pair of weeks passed. July turned to August, and Lynn worked sporadically, running each morning and venturing beyond the shelter of her Queens apartment with increasing confidence and steadily expanding horizons, learning to be a woman.

The anxieties of the murder, her connectedness with it, and exposure by the investigating officers faded as she heard no more from the police. She had thought little of the detective and aspiring writer and so was again surprised one evening when she answered a knock on her door and found him standing outside her apartment.

"Is this an official visit, Detective?" she asked with some antagonism. "You realize visits from the police are a bit disconcerting. Is there some change in the case?"

"No," Anderson answered, "that's pretty much concluded." He produced a large manila envelope he had been carrying under one arm. "I have a story I've written. You said you would be willing to read it."

Lynn stepped aside and directed her guest into the parlor.

"Yes," she said with relief sufficient to qualify as amusement. "I did, and I shall."

She took the envelope and placed it on her desk. Turning to confront her visitor, who had followed her into the apartment, she discovered his gaze to be fixed on the envelope. "Did you want me to read it now?"

Anderson looked at her intently. "I had hoped you would."

Lynn sat on the desk chair, crossed her legs, tugging the hem of her short skirt down.

"Are you on duty, Detective Anderson?" she asked.

The question apparently caused some confusion. "No, why do you ask?"

"I just thought you might be. You seem to be still in uniform."

Anderson glanced down at his suit. "I see. I do generally dress this way, and even off duty I'm still a policeman. That never changes. Is that what you meant?"

"Yes, I guess so." Lynn picked up the hefty envelope. "Well, Detective, I'm somewhat hesitant to read this with you watching like a vulture from my sofa. That would make me even more nervous than you already do."

"I make you nervous?"

"Of course you do. You're a policeman, and," she indicated her appearance, "as your partner made clear, I'm not exactly a member of mainstream society."

The officer's tone turned official. "You've established you're under medical care. Do you commit acts of prostitution?"

"Certainly not."

"Then you are violating no laws. You have nothing to fear from the police." As Lynn had done, Anderson made a gesture encompassing her appearance. "Apparently you go out like this, do you not?"

"Yes," Lynn answered, "I live this way full time. It's part of the process."

"Have you experienced any difficulties?"

Growing uncomfortable with what seemed to be an interrogation, Lynn shifted on her chair, uncrossing her legs. "Other than when your perceptive partner discerned the truth, I've been living as a female with general success. Is this some sort of investigation now?"

Anderson leaned back on the couch and seemed to transform from policeman to civilian. "I didn't mean to give that impression," he said in a much more congenial tone. "It's more curiosity. Most cross-dressers I've encountered have been turning tricks in some parking lot or alley. You're quite a new experience."

"Well, technically, Detective, I'm not really a cross-dresser."

"I understand that there are varied classifications. My point is that you are making a living producing work like that book rather than on the street. I find that intriguing."

"I'm pleased I can amuse." Lynn rose and walked to the door.

"I didn't say *amusing*," the policeman quickly countered.

"Quite right," Lynn conceded. "You no doubt have, Detective, off-duty times. When is your next one?"

The policeman followed Lynn to the door. "I'm off Friday."

"Have you plans for then?"

"No, no plans."

Lynn opened the door for the detective to pass to the landing. "Then stop by that evening about eight o'clock. I promise I will have read your work, though once again, I am by no means a critic, teacher, or guru."

"Understood. I'll be here."

Lynn walked out onto the landing and, leaning over the railing, watched Anderson pound down the stairway. When she heard the lobby door shut, she went back inside, picked up the manila envelope and considered it briefly, then set it aside and went back to work.

5.

Two days later, at 8 P. M. on another warm evening, the detective reappeared at Lynn's door. Though still wearing an officious, subdued suit and tie, his pleasant greeting seemed hardly official. Lynn welcomed him and directed him once more to her couch.

"You're prompt, Detective," she began. "As promised, I've read your story, and..."

"Wait," Anderson interrupted. "I'd prefer to face the guillotine on a full stomach. I haven't had dinner yet, and I'm starving. I thought maybe we could get something to eat before you destroy my hopes."

Lynn was stunned. "Dinner? Out?"

"Have you eaten?"

"No, but do you really want me to go outside with you? Like this?"

"You said you live this way. You go about the city."

"Yes, but..." Lynn stammered in confusion, then squinted questioningly at the policeman. "Is this some sort a bribe?"

"That's not a funny word to a policeman." Seeing that Lynn remained skeptical, Anderson sought to explain. "About dinner, um..." he struggled to find a proper form of direct address.

"Lynn." She shot it out. "How about trying 'Lynn?"

"Lynn." It appeared to be a painful effort. "I'm serious. I'd like a professional critique of my work. I want some of your time and I don't expect you to just donate it. I know professionals charge considerably for such service, so I'll buy you dinner. And I am hungry."

"Reward for any advice I can give would be payment received under false pretenses." Her gentle attempt at humor signaled growing acceptance of the unexpected and odd situation.

Anderson persisted. "It's well past dinner time."

"You're serious."

"I am."

Lynn considered for a few seconds, then decided to plunge on in.

"Alright, then. Where? Nick's?"

"Certainly not. I don't recreate in my own precinct. This is where I work. I have my car outside, and we can go to a place I know in Brooklyn."

"Wait here. Give me a few minutes to get ready." She walked into the bedroom alcove, closing it off with the screen as she entered. Above the sound of the armoire doors and dresser drawers opening and shutting, she called out to the detective. "There are some beers and pop in the 'fridge. Help yourself."

Several minutes later she folded the screen aside to reveal herself in a short, belted black dress and high-heeled shoes. Her developing breasts provided a subtle, but unmistakable curve to the bodice of her dress.

"Acceptable?" she asked the policeman who, she discovered, had accepted her invitation to have a beer.

Without comment, he emptied the bottle, rose, and went into the kitchen area to dispose of it.

"Under the sink," Lynn advised, seeing him look about for the garbage can. She noticed his attention linger over several bottles of pills placed next to the sink. "I'm not a druggy, Detective. Those are what are making me become what I am…becoming. They're hormones and legally prescribed."

"Sorry," he answered, dropping the beer bottle into the can beneath the sink. "I wasn't meaning to snoop. Shall we go?" Ignoring Lynn's disbelieving scowl, he walked to the door, stepped out onto the landing and began descending the stairs.

Lynn turned, after locking her apartment door, to see the policeman far below, heading down the stairs past the darkened offices that occupied the two floors below hers. Accepting that he was not waiting for her, she followed, catching up with him on the sidewalk. Though it was not yet dark, the sun had long since set below the city skyline and shadowy evening had settled into the quiet Long Island City neighborhood.

The policeman paused long enough to point out his car before walking around to the street side and getting in. Lynn stood at the curb beside the car, and Anderson reached over and pushed open the passenger door.

"Hop in," he said. "It wasn't locked."

Resigned to being denied a well-mannered deference, Lynn stepped into the car. "I was sort of expecting you to open the car door for me. It would help."

"Help?" The detective's attention was devoted to the sparse traffic on the boulevard.

"With the image."

"Ah, I get it." He put the car in gear, checked for traffic, and pulled out. At the end of the boulevard he blew through a stop sign and turned left onto Jackson Avenue.

"I guess officialdom can get away with that," Lynn commented on his indifference to traffic laws. "Where are we going?"

"There's a restaurant I know in Brooklyn Heights. Under the bridge. It's quiet and..."

"Dark, no doubt," Lynn finished his thought.

Anderson looked at her for the first time since she had entered the car and smiled. "It is kind of dark. I'm sure you'll like it."

He drove quickly, aggressively, east to the Pulaski Bridge, crossing over into Brooklyn and onto the Brooklyn-Queens Expressway. He concentrated on driving, and Lynn, a bit unsettled by his speed, didn't speak until they had exited the expressway near the Brooklyn Bridge and parked on a secluded, tree-lined residential street tucked into the shadow of the towering and historic bridge.

"The restaurant is just around that corner," Anderson pointed ahead through the deeper darkness to the lights of a more vibrant and commercial cross street. He got out of the car and began walking along the sidewalk until, realizing that he was alone, he stopped and looked back. Lynn remained seated in the car. She waved at the uncomprehending detective, then, as he made no move to retrieve her, got out of the car and joined him.

"You know," she said as they walked together toward the corner, "you might want to consider that we would be more convincing if you were to act as though you're out with a woman rather than one of your drinking buddies. Wait for me, open doors. That sort of thing."

Anderson considered this. "You might be right," he conceded.

They reached the corner, turned right, and the policeman stopped before the heavy wooden door of an Irish Pub. Amazingly, he held the door open for Lynn, who preceded him into the darkness of a tavern and restaurant dominated by a massive flag of Ireland hanging behind the bar. She waited, assessing the Irish décor, while Anderson, apparently a familiar customer, spoke with a welcoming waiter. When her companion started off behind their guide, leaving her behind again, she rather loudly cleared her throat.

The policeman turned around. "Oh, yeah. Sorry again." He paused to allow Lynn to go ahead of him, and the waiter led them to a rather secluded table in the rear of the room, held out a chair for Lynn and, when Anderson had seated himself across from her, placed menus before them, and invited drink orders.

"I'll have a beer," Anderson said, and he was immediately struck in the shin by Lynn's shoe.

She looked directly at the detective. "I'll have a Vodka and 7Up," she snarled.

"Oh, yes," Anderson recovered. "A beer and a Vodka and 7Up."

When the waiter had departed, Lynn leaned across the table and spoke softly. "Once, earlier this evening, I got you to refer to me as 'Lynn.' I greatly appreciated that and hope you continue to do so. It's a bit awkward, though, to have to address you as 'Detective Anderson.' Is there some more informal name I could use?"

"Michael."

"Michael." Lynn repeated the name. "Michael Anderson. Not 'Mike?"

"Nope. It's always been Michael."

Conversation came to a halt, but before the silence became uncomfortable, the waiter arrived with their drinks and prepared to take their orders for dinner. Anderson ordered what Lynn assumed, as he had not looked at the menu, was his standard fare. Feeling pressured, she quickly scanned her own menu and chose her dinner.

"So, Michael," determined to avoid further awkward silence, Lynn introduced the evening's topic, "I've read your story and I'm impressed. Perhaps even 'surprised." She alluded with a hint of sarcasm to the detective's difficulty accepting that she wrote as she did.

The policeman leaned forward, eager to hear more. "You think it's good?"

"I do. There are some points I'd like to make, some ideas you might want to consider."

"Like what?" Anderson's voice mixed excitement with disappointment.

"Well, there are several ideas I'd like to share. You must understand, though, that I'm not claiming to be some sort of teacher or authority."

"You've made that point more than clear. What ideas?"

"Mostly mechanical concerns: structure, characterization, dialog. Just general concepts."

"What's left? That may be general, but it sounds pretty comprehensive. Did I have anything right?"

Lynn smiled at the detective's rather insecure sensitivity.

"It's not that serious, Michael. Fine tuning, really. I made some pencil notes in the margins of your pages. We could go over those."

The policeman began to press further, but just then the waiter reappeared and began placing dishes on the table.

Lynn leaned back, looked down at herself in an almost unconscious assessment and appreciation of her appearance. She crossed her legs and, looking her companion, observed, "Dinner is here. I suggest we dispense with business until after we have eaten."

"But..."

Lynn stopped him. "You suggested this dinner was payment for my time, so I'm going to insist that we do no work during it. Just have pleasant conversation. Besides, it would really be more effective to have the notes before us."

Reluctantly, he agreed.

"So, then," Lynn began as they embarked on their meal, "You're a New York cop, but I'm guessing, by your speech, that you're not originally from New York."

"I'm not," he confirmed Lynn's assumption. "I'm from a very small town in Idaho, just in the foothills of the mountains."

"As I thought." Lynn pointed triumphantly with her fork. "Well, not about Idaho exactly, but you certainly don't speak like a native New Yorker. I imagine it's a beautiful place, your hometown."

"It is."

"I've never been to Idaho. I'd love to see your town."

Anderson concentrated on his meal. "That's unlikely."

"Yes, I suppose it is." Somewhat crestfallen, Lynn leaned back and glanced down at her legs.

"Why are you doing that?" The fact that he had, apparently without looking up from his dinner, noticed Lynn's act of self-assessment testified to his predisposition for alert observation. "You keep looking at yourself. Is something wrong?"

"No." Lynn sat up straight, uncrossed her legs, and skootched herself closer to the table. "I'm sorry. I don't often find myself in this situation; it's a pleasant experience, and I was simply enjoying it. It won't happen again." Shifting gears, she returned to the policeman's history. "Do you still have family in Idaho?"

"Yes." Anderson held up his beer in response to the waiter's unspoken inquiry.

Lynn, resigned to acting on her own behalf, indicated that she was content with her drink and when the waiter had departed, she launched an inquiry of her own. "You're not married." It was as much a question as a statement.

For the first time since he had begun eating, Anderson focused on Lynn. "Why do you ask? It's not pertinent. Besides, who would marry someone with this boxer's mug?"

"You box?"

"Just amateur." Anderson resumed attacking his meal.

"You have a good face."

"Is there anything wrong with your meal?" Anderson conveyed his annoyance.

"It's possible to converse and eat simultaneously, Michael. And, I'm sincere," Lynn insisted. "You have a very kind face. That's important. There is compassion in your face. It's very attractive."

The policeman put down his utensils and looked intently at Lynn. "Could we drop this? I'm aware that I'm not handsome. I harbor no illusions, nor do I need self-esteem building. Also, if I were married, I would not be doing this. Though," he added as an afterthought, "I guess it wouldn't really be cheating." He softly chuckled at what he apparently found humorous.

"What do you mean?"

"It's not like you're a real woman," Anderson whispered this last.

Lynn looked away. "That's true. And I didn't say 'handsome,' I said attractive. The two aren't necessarily the same."

After another uncomfortable pause, Lynn revisited Anderson's allusion to gender imperfection. "You know," she began, "oddly enough, you've made a point a man I knew in Chicago took: I'm not real. He could spend time with me and not be cheating on his wife."

"That's absurd."

"He had a point, I guess. It seemed to work for him."

Again Anderson diverted some attention from consumption of his meal.

"What did he want with you?"

"That's a bit crude, even for a policeman, don't you think?"

Anderson merely shrugged and returned to devouring his meal. "So you're gay, too?" he managed between bites to suggest more than ask.

"Crude and personal as well." Lynn put down her fork and glowered at the inattentive officer.

Soon Anderson noticed the ponderous silence and looked up. "I didn't intend to be crude. It seems a natural observation."

They each resumed eating, but Lynn found herself unable to give the detective a pass.

"O. K.," she reasserted herself, "gay or not gay." She leaned forward and spoke in a whisper to keep the conversation confined to their table. "It may not be that simple. I like to think that sexual expression is properly conducted between the two genders. It's just that I have been able to be either one. More particularly this one, of late. And as for the married gentleman, though it's not a topic for discussion here, I was willing to participate in activity his wife wouldn't."

She watched to see if all this had any effect on the policeman, but he had no response and in fact gave little indication that he had ingested Lynn's statement, apparently ingesting only his meal. He paused from that activity for a drink of beer and used the moment to inquire further of Lynn's background.

"Not gay, then, and you're from Chicago. How long have you been in New York?"

Welcoming the change of topic and Anderson's apparent interest in less awkwardly personal matters, Lynn responded happily. "Not too long. I moved into my apartment last March, on the spring equinox."

"Why?"

The question perplexed Lynn. "Why the equinox?"

"No," Anderson clarified, "why move to New York?"

Lynn glanced around the room to reassure herself that no one had been overhearing their conversation, then took a sip from her drink. "That's a bit complex. You said you don't understand me. Well, I wasn't really understanding myself. As a male I'd been involved with women, nearly engaged once, actually; and as a female I was active with men. My married friend suggested I needed to make a decision. I began hormone therapy, and as I grew more feminine, it became increasingly difficult to conduct my life around my family and friends, so I came to New York. 'If you can make it here, you can make it anywhere,' as the song says."

"Then you've made a decision."

"It seems so. At least for now."

"You could reverse it?"

"I could. It would take some time to return to being as I had been, but I could. Is this of some professional interest?"

Anderson shrugged and returned to his meal. "Just curiosity. You said you wanted conversation."

He signaled the waiter for two more drinks, remembering at last to include his guest, and, resupplied, embraced a less intense conversation, one concerned with the summer, the weather, New York heat, and similar inoffensive dinner table topics. Upon questioning, he was surprised to discover Lynn to be a knowledgeable and active sports fan, though he found fault with her stable of favorite teams, none of which called New York home.

When they were through eating and he had paid the bill, they stepped back into the Brooklyn night and the glare of streetlamps. Upon turning the corner into the more sheltering darkness of the residential street, Anderson reopened the significant object of his interest in Lynn.

"Dinner is over," he rather jarringly began. "What can you tell me about my story?"

"I told you, Michael, that I have notes. If you want this done right, we'll need to have them and your story in front of us. Take me home, and we can get to work."

"I don't mean to seem pushy," the policeman offered a tepid apology. "You have to understand how important this is to me. Important enough that I can..." he abruptly cut off his speech.

"That you can overcome your disgust," Lynn offered a possible close to his sentence. "I appreciate your courage."

"Not disgust. Just uncertainty, unfamiliarity."

"You seem to have an understanding of the shades of transgender forms. Surely in your official capacity you encounter people like me."

"Not like you. The crossdressers and trannies I meet have come in contact with me in very unpleasant circumstances. You are the first..." he struggled for an apt adjective, "reasonable one I've met."

By the time Anderson had concluded this observation, they had arrived at his parked car, and once again Lynn stood outside while he got into the driver's seat.

"Oops," he said, reaching across to push open the passenger door.

Lynn passed the extremely rapid return trip to Long Island City in anxious silence. To her surprise, added to her relief at getting home safely, when Anderson had parked his car in front of her apartment, he jumped out, raced around the vehicle, and opened the door.

"Very gracious," she congratulated Anderson as she stepped out, consciously enjoying the look and feel of her legs in the tight skirt, but unable to detect any interest from the policeman. She led the way up the two flights of stairs and, once inside the apartment, walked into the kitchen alcove.

"Would you like a beer while we go over this?" she asked.

Responding affirmatively, Anderson followed her into the narrow space between the sink and stove on one side and the refrigerator on the other.

"I think I actually have a pair of beer mugs up here somewhere," Lynn said, reaching up to search through a cabinet above the stove. "Grab two beers out of the 'fridge, would you, while I look for them?"

She struggled to search through glassware on the top shelf and, upon locating the mugs, triumphantly exclaimed, "Success. I have them."

With one mug in each hand she pushed the cabinet door shut and, keeping her hands above her head to facilitate turning around in the narrow space with Anderson just behind her, she was started to discover the detective facing her and, in the narrow confines, extremely close.

"Ah," she stammered, "here are the ..."

Her announcement was summarily cut off when Anderson seized her by her waist, pulled her close, trapping her arms above her head, and kissed her. Stunned, she recoiled just momentarily without actually struggling, then accepted the embrace, surrendering to the sensual rush. When she sought to lower her arms to return the detective's embrace, however, he suddenly pushed her away. He leaned back against the unopened refrigerator, staring at her with a look of horror.

"I've got to go," he said tersely and walked rapidly out of the kitchen alcove.

"Go?" Lynn was uncomprehending, but Anderson, ignoring her, fled out of the door, slamming it closed behind him.

Lynn followed him, reaching the landing in time to see his head disappear around the turn of the stairs below. She leaned over the railing and listened to her supposed pupil's thundering flight down to the lobby. When the outer door slammed shut as firmly as had her own apartment door, she turned back from the stairwell and reentered her home.

"Fudge," she said to the empty dwelling. Presently she discovered that she still held the two beer mugs, and after a brief and disappointed study of them, she dejectedly walked back to the kitchen and returned them to the cabinet.

6.

August approached September, and the heat of the summer increased. At mid-day along some streets of Long Island City, particularly those near the river, the fetid smell of decaying garbage rose with the heat from the pavement. Lynn began running in the evening, just at the beginning of a false twilight when the sun, though still well above a natural horizon, began to disappear behind the Manhattan towers, affording, if not coolness, at least less oppressive heat.

Enjoying the consistent effort for its spiritual benefits as well as for the physical stress necessary for preserving a thin body, she had continued increasing her distances, soon able add to the northernmost extent of her run a leg across the 59th Street Bridge to Manhattan and back, and on a particularly hot evening she struggled the last few blocks of the home stretch along Vernon Boulevard. Reaching for breath in the heated air, she looked ahead to the final goal, seeking encouragement for the finish, and through the sweat and exhaustion she discerned a familiar car parked in front of her building. Struggling past another intersection, she focused on the vehicle and confirmed that it was Detective Anderson's. She considered turning into a side street, but, hot and tired, decided to confront the policeman. She hit her finish line in the block before her own and walked, cooling down, toward her home.

As she crossed the last street before her building, she saw the silhouetted man in the driver's seat get out of the car and, leaning on its roof, watch her approach. She came alongside the car and, ignoring its owner, turned to the building wall and began to stretch out. As a final effort, she spread her feet apart and bent over at the waist, looking back between her legs at the parked car across the top of which the policeman remained watching her. Done, she turned to face the detective.

"Do you still have that beer?" he asked.

Lynn contemplated him momentarily before answering. "Someone drank it, but I have some new ones. Are you coming up?"

Anderson removed his arms from the car roof and walked around to the building entrance. Lynn stepped past him, leading the way up to her home. Inside, she pulled off the band that secured her ponytail and shook her hair loose.

"You know where the beer is. Help yourself - again - and make yourself comfortable. I'm a sweaty mess and need a shower. I won't be long."

A quarter of an hour later she stepped out of the bathroom wrapped in a large towel hooked just under her armpits. Her visitor stood at the edge of the kitchen drinking from a bottle of beer.

"No mug?" Lynn's sarcasm was ignored. "Where's mine?"

Anderson produced another open bottle from the counter, and Lynn walked over to take it. She took a long drink and then confronted her guest. Neither spoke, but the policeman placed his beer on the counter, reached one arm around Lynn's waist, and pulled her close.

"This is when you exited last time," she pointed out.

"I know. It was a bit of a shock. I've been giving considerable thought to it."

"It?"

"You. What you are. What I had to have been thinking. You're convincing enough that I guess I just forgot." He drew Lynn still closer and bent down to kiss her.

As the kiss continued longer that the previous one, Lynn felt the one part of her that remained David begin to respond. When Anderson placed the fingers of one hand inside the top of her towel and began to pull, she abruptly stopped him.

"Don't," she grabbed his hand. "I'm naked." She pulled away. "I don't want you to see me naked. It would spoil everything. Wait just a minute."

She ran behind the bedroom screen, quickly returning still wrapped in the towel, apparently unchanged, and pressed back against the detective, reaching one arm around his neck and with her other hand placed his back at the top of the towel.

"Now you may resume."

"I don't see any difference," Anderson said.

"It's just the difference that I don't want you to see." She kissed him and thrilled with excitement as he pulled the towel free and let it drop to the floor. She stood before him wearing only a pair of black panties.

As they kissed, Anderson slipped a hand down to one of her breasts, gently feeling it and seeking its nipple.

Lynn leaned back. "They're small, I know, but they're growing."

Playing with the nipple of Lynn's left breast, with his other hand Anderson grasped the hair at the base of her neck and turned her face up, but as he pulled her face toward his, he glanced down at her crotch. She noticed and wrenched herself free, turning her back to him and pulling his arms around her.

"Don't look down there," she pleaded. "I can satisfy you without that part of me."

Releasing one of his arms, she led him to her bed and sat, pulling him after her. She turned her legs together to one side to hide, as much as possible, the growing bulge in her panties. Reaching up to his neck, she pulled his suit coat down and, with his cooperation, off his arms. Kissing him fervently, she reached both hands down to his belt buckle, but stopped abruptly when she encountered the equipment on his belt.

"I assumed you were off duty." She expressed surprise.

"I told you we're never really off duty. I always carry these."

He removed his weapon and badge, placing them on the floor beside the bed. Lynn then returned to her work on the lightened belt. Having loosened it, she helped him remove his tie, shirt, and T-shirt, revealing a hairy, taught, and well-muscled chest. She rose up on her knees and wrapped her arms around his neck, pressing his lips to her breasts. Though she sensed some struggle, some resistance, in Anderson's response, she also felt his excitement growing more intense, as was her own. She opened his pants and slowly moved down his body.

Some minutes later the detective sat on the edge of Lynn's bed, his head held in his hands. Lynn lay beside him. Though unlit by direct sunlight, the apartment was bathed in the sterile glow of the skyscrapers across the river, a softened light that penetrated into the bedroom alcove. Anderson's profile was silhouetted, and Lynn studied the sadness of his expression.

"Listen, Michael," she said, "I can imagine what you're feeling. To a great extent it's just post-orgasmic depression. Like buyer's remorse. You seemed to enjoy that; it must have been pleasurable."

"Yes," the policeman spoke softly without turning his head. "It was, but now I'm left with what it means. It's not really normal. You're not a real..."

Lynn sat up. "Don't say it. I know what I'm not."

Anderson did not respond. Lynn watched him for a moment, then spoke again. "I'm glad you enjoyed it, Michael," she said, "but now I need your help."

"My help?" He remained motionless.

"I'm all wound up. I need to come, too."

"I won't do what you did."

"I wouldn't want you to. That would destroy the illusion. All you have to do is lie on top of me, between my legs. Play with my breasts. I can do the rest."

Still the policeman sat with his head in his hands. Lynn took his hands and pulled them toward her, leaning back on the bed. Anderson resisted, but eventually allowed her to slip one leg on the other side of his body and bring him with her as she lay down. When she had finished, Anderson rolled off of her and resumed his seat on the edge of the bed. Spent, fulfilled, Lynn worked on coming down, stretching out the experience until the detective reached for his clothes.

"So you're bolting again?"

He just glanced at her and continued collecting and getting into his clothes.

"Will I see you again?" she asked.

"I don't know. I'm not thinking clearly."

"Perhaps when you're feeling horny again." There was bitterness in her tone.

"That's certainly part of it," Anderson unashamedly admitted, "but not all. I don't go out with many women. I don't exactly attract them. Astoundingly enough, you would be the most beautiful woman I've ever been with."

"I'd like to think of that as being something other than 'astounding.'"

"But you're not..." He stopped. "I can't believe I've done this. I'm not queer."

"That's not supposed to be the nature of this situation," Lynn argued. "I have no desire to have sex with someone of my own gender. I'm not even as attracted to males as much as I am to being female. Males greatly assist that."

"But you're not female."

"I'm getting there."

Anderson ignored that idea and continued getting dressed. Frustrated, disappointed, Lynn watched him, but as he stood up and put on his suit coat, she had an inspiration.

Listen," she grabbed his arm, "Let's put this aside. I still have your story. We haven't looked at my notes." She stood up beside him. "Let me get dressed, and we can have some more beers and go over your writing."

He waivered. She pressed her apparent advantage.

"After all, that's what you came here for in the first place. You paid for it with a dinner. It's a sunk cost, and it's still early. We can be just teacher and pupil. No fooling around. No complications." She felt the hook sink in. "I have some really good ideas for you."

A tense moment passed, then Anderson relented.

"O. K.," he said without much enthusiasm.

"Yes!" Lynn exclaimed as she pushed the detective out of the alcove and reached into her armoire for a dress.

7.

Relieved of the pressures of complex and murky sexual passions, Lynn and the detective spent several hours that evening studying his story and discussing her notes and comments. Each enjoyed and profited from the nascent pupil/tutor relationship, and in the following two weeks they continued meeting and writing together, the detective phoning when he could make available an off-duty evening, and Lynn waiting for the calls that came, with September, once or twice a week.

The time proved exceedingly productive for both. Lynn delivered a long overdue novel to her agent, and the detective not only revised his story, but also acquired the courage to submit it to a magazine. The novel was declined by two publishers, and the story rejected by the magazine, but if the pair failed of achieving immediate literary success, they did succeed in establishing a comfortable pattern for working together. They made no allusion to the physical intimacy that had preceded their initial collaboration, a silence that probably served the detective more than it did Lynn, who found herself unable to dismiss the incident as unrepeatable.

One particularly hot and humid night in early September they worked unusually late, Lynn wearing a light, ankle length skirt and sitting cross-legged on the floor, the skirt drawn up her legs and crumpled between them, a pose that she had seen Sophia Loren strike in a movie and that she had envied and emulated.

"That's it for me," she said suddenly to Anderson, who, sitting on the couch and concentrating on his act of creation, ignored her and furiously continued pouring words into the notebook he held on his lap.

Lynn watched him for a few moments, then rose and walked to the open window. She pressed her head against the glass of the upper pane and looked out at the lights across the river. "Let's go up on the roof," she suggested. "It has to be cooler up there."

Unperturbedly hunched over his work, Anderson continued to ignore her. Frowning with heat and impatience, Lynn jumped over the back of the couch, landing beside the intensely focused policeman with a jarring force that knocked the writing pad from his lap.

"What?" he asked with no small amount of annoyance.

"Come on," Lynn cajoled. "Let's go up on the roof. It's too hot in here. I can't work anymore tonight." She pulled on his arm. "Come up on the roof with me. We can watch the boats. Enough work for one night."

Though the dogged determination that served him as a detective also informed his approach to writing, Anderson yielded to Lynn's request. He retrieved his notebook from the floor, but set it aside and followed her through the window and up the ladder to the upper roof. Stepping over the low parapet, he continued to trail behind her to the front of the building where she had placed her mattress. Lynn pulled the protecting plastic sheeting from the mattress and flopped down, leaving room for Anderson to lie down beside her.

The detective, though, remained standing, looking about the panoramic view of Queens stretching away to the east and the black line of the East River separating their quiet, dark rooftop from the world's most brilliant and recognizable urban skyline. He peered over the roof edge at the street below, apparently lost in thought.

"You're being a detective, aren't you?" Lynn observed. "Thinking about what I could have seen that night."

"No," he said, "I'm watching something interesting occurring right now. Look."

As she had the night of the killing, Lynn raised her head above the low wall edging the roof and looked below at the virtually deserted street. Following Anderson's direction, she saw, staggering out of the park at the south end of the boulevard, an obviously inebriated man apparently heading for "Bellomini's Tavern."

"It's past that bar's licensed closing time," the policeman observed, "yet I bet he gets in."

"He will if he's a local," Lynn suggested."

Unaware of the two rooftop spies observing him, the man eventually located the darkened tavern's door and knocked on the small window. When the curtain covering the window was pulled aside, a shaft of eerily green light shown out onto the pavement, casting a pale shadow of the man onto the sidewalk. As suddenly as the curtain had been pulled aside, it was replaced. The door opened, the late night tippler was gathered into the illicitly operating tavern, and the door shut behind him.

"I ought to go down there and bust that place," Anderson grumbled.

"Oh, please," Lynn was dismissive. "I understand "Bellomini's" has been open twenty-four hours a day since Peter Munuit conned the Indians out of Manhattan. Your precinct house is just around the corner. Generations of cops have looked the other way. You've probably stopped in there for a beer after hours yourself."

The policeman's guilty grin was sufficient confession. "Still," he argued, "someday it should be stopped."

Lynn lay back on the mattress, stretching her arms out from her body and focusing on the infinite panorama drifting above. Anderson turned his attention to the lights of Manhattan.

"Am I a writer?" he asked.

"That came from nowhere."

"Not really. It's why I'm here. Am I?"

Lynn's answer came after moments of consideration, and it failed to satisfy. "I don't know, Michael. Who is? There are great ones that are never read and absolute abominations that have made millions. I like your work. I like my work, but I'm not sure we're writers."

"You are." Anderson finally sat down on the mattress to more intently pursue his inquiry. "You're published. You're making a living."

Lynn smirked. "Again, one book of short stories does not a career make. I'm living on greeting card pennies and money I saved in Chicago and that's running short. And I'm not certain I'm being much help to you."

"Then what do you recommend? Should I take classes?"

"In my opinion the best teachers are the masters. You should read the works of the great ones and pay attention to how they did what they did."

"Like who? Hemmingway?"

The suggestion sat Lynn up beside her pupil. "Not Hemmingway. And it's *whom.* I know he's all the rage, but he'll fry your talent. Obviously," she calmed herself, "this is opinion, but you should study 'The Master,' Henry James. Have you read any Henry James?"

Anderson admitted he had not, that he was unaware of the author.

"O. K.," Lynn warmed to her subject. "Probably you've heard of *The Turn of the Screw.* It's his most accessibly popular work, but he has many novels any one of which is a worthwhile study. You know what?" Mention of Henry James triggered a recollection. "This is great. There's an exhibit of James' holographs, his handwritten manuscripts, at the library on 42"[d] Street. Go look at it. You'll be able to see his actual writing. Then check out a book of his, probably one of his shorter works for a start. Lesson over."

She lay back down on the mattress, and the two pursuers of literature quietly studied the lights across the river, a view that triggered for Lynn a popular culture allusion.

"In this city," she adopted a mocking dramatic tone, "we certainly have sufficient and fertile ground for story ideas. 'There are eight million stories in the Naked City. This has been one of them.'"

Anderson looked down. "Eight million stories? Where did you get that?"

"The television show." Lynn was surprised that he seemed unfamiliar with her quotation. "'Naked City.' That's its closing line. Or something like it."

The policeman continued to convey incomprehension.

"Fine," she said with some exasperation, "Like this," she sat up and pulled off her blouse, exposing her breasts. "Naked City."

Anderson smiled at the joke. "I was never much of a TV fan." He sat down beside Lynn.

"Have you noticed," she asked, "that they're getting larger?"

"What's getting larger?" The detective looked over at Manhattan, expecting to see the answer to his question there.

Lynn grabbed the collar of his shirt and pulled him toward her. "My breasts," she explained.

"I've noticed."

Lynn took one of Anderson's hands and placed it on her left breast, and unresisting, the policeman caressed it and leaned down to kiss her.

The following morning, as the indirect light of the rising sun slowly illuminated Lynn's apartment, there seemed to be no remorse in the detective as he sat on her couch. Acceptance of the sexual aspect of their relationship, however, failed to develop into a thorough embracing of it, and the two lovers sat at separate ends of the sofa, Lynn reprising her Sophia Loren pose.

"It's morning," Anderson identified the obvious. "I should go."

Disappointedly suspicious of one implication of this announcement - that the policeman retained a reluctance to be with her in the glare of daylight - Lynn nonetheless said nothing, content with finding progress in the fact that he had not immediately fled at the conclusion of their love making, as she was able to characterize it. He made, however, no motion to leave.

"I wonder," he hesitated, apparently searching for a way to introduce some concern.

"Yes?"

He plunged in. "Remember those pictures from Vietnam?"

"Of course. They are, after all, mine."

"Well, I wonder. You soldiered with those men, fought beside them. Presumably you slept with them." He looked directly at Lynn. "Did you want to screw them?"

Lynn folded her arms beneath her breasts, tempering, before speaking, the surprise and mild anger with which she met this new topic. "I'm not sure this is fair, Michael." She hesitated, framing her answer. "Presumably you mean 'slept beside them.' No, I never had sexual thoughts about them. I was one person then, although," she realized the potential for being misleading, "I have always been this way," indicating her appearance, "always. For much of my life I've stifled it, been able to compartmentalize it. There was no room for it during the time in Vietnam, so it was deeply buried. It didn't intrude. I've kept the two lives separate. Hardly anyone who knows of David is aware of me, I believe."

It was unclear whether or not the answer satisfied Anderson's need. He had no response, but his quietude did not seem to Lynn to derive, as had previous silence, from disgust and frustration preceding abrupt retreat. She reached a hand to one of his, and he did not withdraw.

"I understand," treading carefully, she continued, "that this relationship... interaction," she adjusted her term in response to a swift and unambiguous glance from the policeman, "is difficult for you. Other women, the real women with whom you've..."

"There haven't been any. I told you once that you are the most beautiful woman I've ever spent time with, and consider the irony of that."

"There haven't been any?"

"I've never had a relationship, as you put it, with a woman. I've paid for sex, but I've never had even a girl friend, not in high school, college, or now."

"Wait a minute." Incredulous, Lynn removed her hand and sat stiffly upright.

"You see me," Anderson said. "I've told you I'm aware I'm goofy looking. I've never been able to talk with a girl or, as an adult, with a woman."

"Don't start with the uglies again. It's not true. You're a bold, confident, strong policeman, Michael. You deal with situations requiring courage and resolute behavior. You don't take any guff."

"My problem has never been with other men. I have no trouble dealing with men. I just can't carry on a conversation with a woman to whom I'm attracted."

"You've never had difficulty talking with me."

Anderson's sarcastic glance required no interpretation.

"O. K.," Lynn conceded and moved on, "we'll let that go. I have to think about this. I feel like I'm in some permutation of *Cyrano De Bergerac*." She dismissed his quizzical expression. "It doesn't matter."

Lynn settled back on the couch and studied both her lover and his revelation. Cognizant that the best course might be to let it all go, she nonetheless yielded to her compulsion to know more. "So there has never been anyone with whom - see, *whom* - you've had a romance?"

"No."

"Not in all of Idaho?"

"I said not." Anderson conveyed the beginning of annoyance. "There was really only one girl I ever really wanted."

"Tell me more."

"Ginny Haliburton."

"Great name. What happened?"

"Nothing."

"Nothing? Something must have happened."

"Nope," Anderson stood his ground. "When I was a Sheriff's Deputy in our county in Idaho, she was one of the dispatchers. I was in love with her."

"And?"

"Other than on official business, I never spoke with her. She was beautiful and popular, and I, of course, was me."

Lynn decided not to wrestle with the grammar. "Go on."

"She married one of the other deputies, and that's when I decided to apply to the New York PD. I was hired and moved here, and that's it."

There seemed to be little more to be said. Tired from their night-long session of study and passion, the two settled into silence as the morning light intensified, losing the soft glow that had rendered the apartment a bit surreal. Eventually the brightness penetrated the detective's consciousness, and he stood up.

"I'm off," he said, but this time he let Lynn hold his arm and accompany him to the door, though a kiss goodbye proved more than he could muster.

"Progress," Lynn said to herself when he had gone, and she walked around the Japanese screen to the bed.

8.

On the morning of the following day, her sleep and work schedule still disrupted by the all-night session, Lynn decided to alter her late summer, heat-beating routine and run before beginning work. Sitting on the floor in the relatively cool living room area of her apartment, she was carefully and thoroughly stretching in preparation for the imminent exercise when a firm knock on her door startled her. She sat motionless, waiting, until a second and equally determined knock convinced her to answer.

Peering through the peephole, she discovered the unexpected Detective Anderson waiting on the landing. As she unlocked the door to let him in, she glanced behind her at the window to confirm that the sun was indeed shining.

"You're here." She greeted him and continued listing the obvious. "The sun's out, it's daylight, and you're here."

"I'm not a vampire, you know."

"Of course, you aren't." Lynn appreciated the pleasant surprise. "This is a first: you in the daylight, and look at you." She indicated his casual attire: blue jeans and an Idaho State University T-shirt. "What's going on?"

As he entered, Anderson held up a partially folded newspaper. "This," he pointed to the paper. This is going on."

Lynn took the paper and studied the article highlighted by the folding. "Winnie the Pooh?" she asked. "Winnie the Pooh is at the public library?"

The policeman snatched the paper back and looked at it, then handed it back to Lynn.

"No, no. Not Winnie the Pooh. Look closer. Below that. Today is the last day of the Henry James exhibit you mentioned. It's closing after today."

Lynn found the notice, but still failed to grasp Anderson's point concerning it.

"Forget Winnie the Pooh," Anderson admonished. "There's the exhibition of illustrations from Winnie the Pooh, but there's also the Henry James one, and it's the last day. I'm off duty. You recommended it, so let's go see it."

She began to grasp what he was suggesting.

"Let's go? You mean you and me?" Looking again to her lone window for one more confirmation of the inconceivable, she questioned the detective's proposal. "You want me to go with you to Manhattan in the daylight? With the sun up?"

"That's what daylight means." It then registered that Lynn was suited up for a run. "I thought you ran in the evening."

"Today I just felt like going in the morning. I'm still disoriented from our all-nighter."

She walked to the kitchen and poured herself a glass of orange juice that she carried over to the window, where she looked out at the shadow of her building thrown toward the city by the morning sun."

"Are you sure?" she asked. "It will be bright daylight. There will be masses of people. Do you really want to be seen with me? You want to take the chance?"

"There's not much chance involved," Anderson argued. "You pass. We're not going to be interviewed for television. Let's go."

After a moment of reflection, Lynn embraced the suggestion. "O. K., be it on your head." She finished her orange juice and practically ran to the bedroom. "Let me get dressed, and we'll be on our way." As she disappeared behind the screen, she offered a compliment. "By the way," she said, "I really like you in something other than your detective suit."

A half-hour later Lynn emerged from the bathroom, makeup in place and wearing a light, spaghetti-strap sundress and a pair of high-heeled sandals.

"Look," she urged Anderson as she stood before him, "you can see cleavage." Receiving no response, she reasserted herself. "Well, you can. What do you know?"

"You've been sarcastic about my dress habits," Anderson suggested, "but you're as much a creature of habit as you accuse me of being. Don't you think those shoes are a bit inappropriate for a summer day library visit? And how about some shorts instead of a dress?"

Lynn looked down at her feet. "I've been waiting for years to dress like this," she defended her choice, "and I don't intend to waste the time I have. I love the sound of high heels as I walk, and dresses and skirts are essential to being female. So, this is it."

Outside on the street Lynn turned toward Anderson's parked car, but he indicated the other direction, toward the park at the end of the boulevard.

"Let's use the subway," he explained. "It's just two quick stops and we're there."

Lynn had to step out quickly to catch up to and then maintain pace with the policeman, who led the way into the morning stream of commuters flowing south to the subway. As they closed in on the park, tributaries from the east and west, from Jackson Avenue and 51st Street, contributed to the flow.

At first Anderson and Lynn could walk beside each other, but as they were swept ever more rapidly toward the gaping mouth of the subway entrance, jostled and bumped by the converging crowds, they struggled to stay together. At the top of the stairway, just as the cascade plunged into the descent to the subterranean station, the possibility of separation became acute, and Anderson reached out and took Lynn's hand. Suddenly oblivious to the chaos surrounding her, Lynn focused on that contact, the first he had initiated in public.

At the bottom of the stairs they pushed aside from the current of regular riders already in possession of their passes, made it to the token booth and bought four tokens. Through the turnstiles and on the platform, then, they fought for position from which to board a train to Manhattan. The wait was short; in moments a Number 7 Line train roared out of the tunnel mouth to their left and screeched to a halt at the station. Lynn and Anderson nudged onto a car, crunched up against each other just inside the door. As suddenly as it had arrived, the train lurched forward, entered the dark tunnel ahead and descended beneath the East River.

The car rolled and tossed as it stormed through the narrow tunnel, and Lynn enjoyed being pressed against the burly policeman who still held her hand. Soon the train began a perceptible ascent and abruptly emerged from the tunnel into the large, brightly lit Grand Central Station stop. When the doors slid open, nearly the entire population of the car swept past Lynn and her companion, who clung to each other and the vertical pole beside them in order to remain on the train. They were able to relax for the most brief of moments before a nearly irresistible wave of commuters flowing in the opposite direction entered the car, forcing them to again brace against the pole to avoid being swept away from the doorway. They held fast to the next station, Bryant Park, the library stop.

Though a bit regretful to no longer be pressed up against Anderson, Lynn was happy to return to the sunlight of the upper world. In the considerably less congested pedestrian traffic, Anderson released Lynn's hand, and a short walk brought them around the corner of the monumental Manhattan Library edifice to the main entrance' expansive concrete stairs, home to romancing couples, readers, street performers, and loungers with no particularly compelling occupation. Inside the building, Lynn's resistance to the policeman's suggestion that she not wear high heels was rewarded, as she thoroughly enjoyed the staccato sound they made on the immaculate marble floor.

Anderson found a directory and learned that the Henry James exhibit was housed in a gallery on an upper floor. He recommended taking an elevator, but Lynn demurred, suggesting that she was receiving far too much pleasure from the sound of her heels and that climbing stairs in her flouncy skirt would be fun.

"That's .. I don't know what," Anderson whispered, "but don't say things like that where someone might hear. It doesn't sound right."

Despite his misgiving, he acceded and they began to climb to the upper floor. With a practiced skill, Lynn was able to watch herself as she climbed, enjoying the experience of being a woman gracefully ascending a dramatic and wide staircase. At the top they arrived at a less ostentatious lobby flanked by two opposing galleries.

"Winnie the Pooh to the left," Lynn pointed out, "and Henry James to the right. What an amusing juxtaposition."

They strode purposefully into the gallery to the right where they paused to collect a brochure and to assess the layout of the exhibition. On either side of a long, straight gallery were waist-high glass cases containing, side-by-side, open books, first editions, and pages of ageing paper covered with flourished, uncluttered handwriting. Plaques with explanatory text stood beside each case, and on the walls of the room were photographs and a few paintings of Henry James and of his notable family.

"Let's begin at the beginning," Lynn suggested, indicating to their left a sign chronicling James' early childhood.

They progressed slowly through the exhibit, carefully studying the holographs and consequent printed texts. Lynn divided her attention between the exhibit and experiencing it as a female. The suggestion of partially exposed breasts as she bent over the cases was thrilling, and she took advantage of ostensibly inadvertent opportunities to press her hips against Anderson. She felt herself to be completely feminine.

She and her companion exchanged observations and comments, and Lynn pointed out aspects of Henry James' work that could be teaching points for them both. One remarkable feature of James' holographs particularly struck her, and, indicating one of the handwritten manuscript pages, she called Anderson's attention to it.

"Look, Michael," she was fervent, "he just wrote. There are hardly any crossings-out. The words just came to him in perfect connection. What a genius. Think about the scrawling messes we make trying to create a first draft."

An hour and a half later they had circumnavigated the gallery, absorbed the lessons of the master. Back at the doorway to the lobby, Lynn stopped and surveyed the exhibit.

"That was magnificent," she gushed. "Let's go back to my place and I'll give you one of his novels. We should get two copies and read it together and discuss it. That's better than any class or workshop."

Visiting the exhibit and the sensuality of experiencing it with her lover left Lynn with a heightened emotional fervor. Unwilling to wait for Anderson to initiate contact, she thrust her arm beneath one of his and grasped his bicep, pressing her body against his as they walked out of the gallery.

As they turned toward the staircase, an arriving family reached the top of the steps and headed toward the Winnie the Pooh exhibit. The mother, hurrying to keep up with her two eager children, followed them through the gallery entrance, but the father lagged a bit behind and as he calmly trailed his family, he glanced toward the Henry James side of the lobby and noticed Lynn and Detective Anderson.

Police Detective Matthews, the indulgent father so unfortunately, for Lynn and Anderson, maintaining his own pace in spite of the exuberance of his children, recognized both his partner and his partner's companion. He flinched perceptibly, only a brief hesitation, but his face clearly, though only momentarily, reflected the shock and disgust he felt. He turned abruptly, without acknowledging his fellow policeman, and disappeared in the wake of his family into the world of Winnie the Pooh.

If disgust had been unmistakable on Matthew's face, dismay was even more evident in Anderson's. The young detective freed himself from Lynn's grasp and charged down the stairway. He plunged ahead unchecked, Lynn hurrying to stay close behind, through the main lobby and out the door. At the top of the expansive stairs, in the heated air and with the frenetic activity of a Manhattan weekday morning surging below and about him, he stopped.

Lynn slowed her pursuit as she pushed through the tall door and saw that Anderson was, if perhaps not waiting, at least no longer racing away. She approached slowly, stood in front of him, but said nothing. His jaw was set, and he stared angrily at the cement beneath his feet.

Without looking up, he suddenly blurted out, "I can't take you home."

With that spat out, he stalked down the stairs, dodging through the maze of library patrons, idlers, and bums, all making use of the commodious staircase.

"Michael," Lynn whispered after the retreating figure, "I'm so sorry."

When he had passed from sight, she slowly followed, no longer attentive to the sound of high heels on cement sidewalk. She traced his path, walking slowly enough to ensure that he would have departed the subway station before she arrived.

9.

Days passed, a week, and with September 21, the summer. The heat, however, remained, and late on the autumnal equinox morning, before the sun reached the western sky and drove the heat in through her window, Lynn sat on the windowsill staring disinterestedly across the river at the Manhattan skyline. Behind her in the shadowy reaches of her apartment, the desk was cluttered with papers, incomplete greeting card messages, unfinished stories, and the blank pages of those yet to be begun.

She had not heard from Detective Anderson and having been given neither his address nor phone number, she could not reach out to him, though she was far from certain it would have been appreciated had she been able to do so.

She held a copy of Henry James' *Portrait of a Lady* in her hand and she had vaguely intended to go up on the roof to read, but had gone no farther than the windowsill. Eventually the sun progressed sufficiently across the sky to protrude beyond the top of the wall above her, shining directly onto the window ledge where she sat. The sudden increase in heat and light put an end to her distraction; she remembered the book in her hand and, accepting that she might just as well fulfill her delayed intention, climbed the ladder to the roof.

Having removed the mattress' protective plastic, Lynn sat on the edge of her rooftop construction, ignoring the book, to gaze over the parapet at the boulevard and neighborhood below. It being time for neither the morning nor the evening commute, and local economic traffic being at best sparse, Vernon Boulevard was calm. From several blocks to the north, however, the approach of a vehicle traveling well above the posted speed limit attracted her attention. She watched with growing interest as the color, make, and model of the car became discernable. When it slowed and pulled abruptly to the curb in front of her building, she confirmed her hope that it was Anderson's and she sprang to her feet, raced across the rooftop and scrambled down the ladder. Undeterred by the crash of her head against the window frame as she hurriedly climbed inside, she ran to the apartment door, but stopped before reaching for the lock to collect herself and pull straight her tank top and short skirt. She opened the door, and outside on the landing stood the startled Anderson.

"Michael," she stepped forward to embrace him, but, uncertain of what to expect, decided to restrain herself.

The policeman was once again without his accustomed detective attire, wearing blue jeans and a different Idaho State University T-shirt. Surprisingly, he grinned broadly at Lynn, displaying none of the misery she had expected.

"May I come in?" he asked.

Though nervous, Lynn regained some composure. "Of course. Certainly." She stepped aside and closed the door as Anderson made his way to the parlor area.

"I'm glad to see you," she began. "I've been worried. Are you all right?"

Anderson remained standing, but smiling, beside the sofa.

"I'm fine," he said. "Things are good."

The two stood in awkward silence. For Lynn, tension and unasked questions hovered about them.

"You're not dressed for work," she ventured. "Are you off duty today?"

"Not exactly," Anderson answered. "I'm not on the force anymore."

Lynn reached out to touch him, but as he made no reciprocal approach, made no contact. "I'm so sorry. Was Matthews vicious? Were you fired?"

"He never even alluded to having seen us. He wasn't exactly friendly the next day, but then, he never really was. And no, I wasn't fired."

Lynn collapsed more than sat onto the sofa, but Anderson remained standing.

"I'm not understanding, then, Michael. Why aren't you on the force?"

"That's what I've come by to tell you. From the moment we parted at the library, I've been trying to put together what in the world I'm doing, and what all this has meant. As I said, Matthews was not a problem, but he made me uncomfortable; the whole thing was hanging over me. I decided I didn't want to go to work everyday with such tension, and that I really needed to face my life. I think this whole incident is going to work out for the better, and you are mostly responsible."

"I know." Lynn looked even more dejected. "I should have refused to go to the library with you. I knew better." She looked up at the apparently now former detective, fearing that forgiveness might be unobtainable.

"Remember," he amusedly suggested, "you said, 'Be it on your head.' You have nothing to be sorry for."

"Could you sit?" she indicated space beside her on the couch.

"I can't really stay long," Anderson declined. "I've got a lot to do today. I really wanted to put your mind at ease, to explain that you've changed my life for the better."

"Really?" Lynn was uncomprehending, but encouraged. "You mean that?"

"Yes. I've learned a lot this summer. For one thing, you've convinced me that I can learn to write."

Lynn moved to the edge of the couch. "You can. And my work has improved during our time. It's been wonderful. But, is that how you are planning on earning a living now? Is that what you're going to do?"

Anderson smiled. "No, of course not. I'm not that deluded. But I wanted to tell you that you're also responsible for my decision to move back to Idaho. I've made..."

Stunned, Lynn interrupted. "Idaho? You're moving back to Idaho?"

"Yes, and as I was saying, I can thank you for that. I've come to realize that I was just running away by coming here. I belong at home. I've made some calls back there and I can have my old job in the Sheriff's Department back. Obviously Ginny Haliburton is no longer available, but there will be other women ..."

"Other women?" Again Lynn interrupted.

"Would you stop doing that? I'm trying to tell you something exciting. Anyway, yes, other women. I've decided you're right: I am bold, confident, resolute, and I don't take any guff from anyone. I don't need to be in fear of women. I can approach anyone, and if they don't like me, that's their loss. You see, I've thought this all through carefully."

Seeing the direction Anderson's epiphany was leading him, Lynn sank back onto the couch, her exhilaration replaced by a sense of impending disaster.

"What's the matter?" Anderson asked, observing Lynn's distress. "This is great, and I owe it all to you."

"You came here to tell me this?" She rose and walked past her guest toward the kitchen.

"I came to thank you. What you've done is amazing."

"And what about us?" she asked, fearing and fairly certain of the answer.

"Us? What do you mean?"

"Nothing, apparently," Lynn muttered too softly for Anderson to hear.

"Do you mean 'us' as in..." He began to understand. "Surely you... I mean, you're not..."

Lynn stomped a foot against the hardwood floor. "I've told you: don't tell me what I'm not." She moved on into the kitchen and leaned against the counter, staring into the sink.

Anderson moved toward her, but stopped before reaching the kitchen alcove.

"I assumed you understood," he sought the right words. "After all, I want to be a father some day, to have a family. You..." He stopped.

"I appreciate your tact, breaking it to me so gently. I should have realized the attraction was limited to some literary guidance and occasional oral sex when you needed it. I shouldn't have read more into it. You've bolted before," she did not lift her focus from the sink. "You know the way. Would you just go?" Lynn waved an arm dismissively in the direction of the doorway. "Just go,"

Anderson hesitated, seeking something more to say, but came up with nothing and so walked to the door and departed.

When his footsteps had ceased sounding down the stairs, Lynn looked up from the sink and at the door Anderson had shut behind him. Distraught, unbelieving, she grasped her lowered head in her hands and leaned her elbows on the counter, staring again into the empty sink. She sought to make her mind blank, to cease thinking, but at the edge of her periphery several small objects beside the sink gradually attracted her attention. She stood up and contemplated the bottles of hormone pills, picked one up and read its label. She picked up another and then a third, studying them all.

"No good. No good," she softly remarked to herself and, using her right foot, pushed open the door of the cabinet beneath the sink. With a swift, decisive motion she swept the pills into the garbage can and walked out of the kitchen.

CHAPTER SEVEN

Return of Spring

A drizzling rain dampened the suburban Chicago grass and perhaps some human spirits, but the May evening promised warmer days to come as David ran from his car across the neatly trimmed lawn to Harry's front porch. The door opened before he could push the doorbell, and his friend eagerly greeted him, reaching out to shake his hand and pull him inside.

"David, this is great. I'm really happy you came. And Christine is excited to see you again."

"I bet."

"No, no. Seriously, David, she is." Harry directed his guest from the entrance foyer to the living room. "She no longer considers you a corrupting influence. I've proved myself to be a solid citizen and impeachable family man now; our marauding days are well behind us both, and when she sees you with your new haircut and suit and tie, she'll have no fear of you leading me astray again."

"I led you astray, you say."

Harry leaned close to whisper. "She likes to think that. I don't discourage it. And she would never have agreed to introduce you to her cousin if she thought you were still a wastrel." Harry leaned even closer to preclude being heard in another part of the house. "Listen, though. You're going to be pleased: my wife's cousin Amy is really hot, and it's getting to be that time of year for you."

"Good Grief," David interrupted, "are you still on about that after all this time?"

"Doesn't matter. She's beautiful, and now I'm going to have to rely on you for some vicarious pleasures. I've told her all about you: war hero and famous writer."

"You're still an idiot, Harry."

"Dinner should be about ready, so have a seat," Harry indicated a sumptuous couch in the perfectly decorated living room, "and I'll go get us each a beer, or rather you a beer -'I'm off the stuff - and get Christine and Amy. Sounds like a comedy duo."

Harry chuckled as he disappeared through a large open doorway beyond which was a formal dinning room and, presumably, the kitchen where his wife and cousin-in-law were busily preparing to entertain their guest.

David declined Harry's invitation to sit and instead walked around the splendidly appointed room, studying various photographs chronicling his friend's adventures in matrimony. He had just about circumnavigated the room when Harry reappeared carrying a glass of beer and another of orange juice.

"Thanks, David offered as he accepted the beer. "Your place is really nice, Harry. I had no idea you had such good taste. The cookie factory must be doing well."

"It is," Harry gave his living room an appreciative survey, "as you'll see when you start work next week. And actually, we rather owe it to you."

"Me?" David was incredulous.

"Yes. Not long after our tennis connection with Mr. Whalen, our sales took off. Apparently Whalen put in the word for us with some other retailers. He'll be thrilled to hear your coming to work with us. No doubt there will be more tennis matches. Which we'll win."

David quietly considered this curious information, and any response was forestalled when Harry's wife entered the living room closely followed by another woman who, David immediately conceded, more than fulfilled Harry's promise.

"David, old buddy," Harry was characteristically enthusiastic, "you remember Christine, and this is her cousin Amy. Amy, my friend David, who has just returned home from harrowing adventures living in New York City to take up the cause of quality cookies."

After a perfunctory embrace with Harry's wife, David shook hands with her cousin, acquiring a growing appreciation of her beauty.

His hosts announced the serving of dinner, and he escorted Amy to the dining room, finding it necessary to begin, in response to her friendly inquiries, disabusing her of the embellishments with which Harry had misled her. He found her calm, rich voice attractive, and as they conversed walking to the dinner table, he studied her graceful and confident stride. He held out a chair, and as Amy swept the skirt of her simple black dress beneath her and took her seat with impeccable ease, David considered how wonderful it would feel to sit just that way in just such a dress.

Acknowledgements

Laura Shabott of the seafaring community Provincetown, Ma. without whose advice, encouragement, enthusiasm, expertise, and guidance *Change of Seasons* would have sunk at the dock.

The People at Orcadian Press who, to employ another metaphor, have shepherded *Change of Seasons* home to the fold.

The Late Lee Brewster who in the 1970's showed a young and hesitant Lynn McDonough that it is possible to exist.

Printed in Great Britain
by Amazon